Tempting the Outlaw

Book 2
Sherwood Forest Shifters

Anna Lowe

Contents

Other books in this series

Sherwood Forest Shifters

Tempting the Sheriff (Book 1)

Tempting the Outlaw (Book 2)

Tempting the Maiden (Book 3)

www.annalowebooks.com

Free Books

Get your free e-books now!

Sign up for my newsletter at *annalowebooks.com* to get three free books!

- *Desert Wolf*: Friend or Foe (Book 1.1 in the Twin Moon Ranch series)

- *Off the Charts* (the prequel to the Serendipity Adventure series)

- *Perfection* (the prequel to the Blue Moon Saloon series)

Chapter One

WILLA

Nottingham, England

December 1193. . .

I pulled at my tight, frilly collar as the carriage lurched along the rutted trail. How had I ever gotten talked into this crazy mission — not to mention this girly outfit?

Beverly peered out the window of the carriage, her eyes darting so quickly, it was a wonder she didn't get dizzy. "Sherwood Forest," she whispered anxiously. "So spooky. So dangerous. . ."

I looked around. Spooky? More like beautiful, especially with rays of wintery sunlight filtering through the trees.

And dangerous? Not if you could handle a weapon. And I was armed to the teeth.

But the only weapon poor Beverly had mastered was feminine charm. I doubt she even recognized the defensive potential in the fan she kept fluttering despite the frosty temperature.

As for me, I wasn't worried about bandits. If anything killed me today, it would be the corset squeezing the air out of my lungs and the itchy collar preventing me from inhaling in the first place. Usually, I wore my long, wavy red hair in a single braid, but now, it was done up so tightly, the skin on my forehead hurt. But making this mission succeed meant looking like a helpless maiden, so I did my best to endure — and imitate Beverly.

How she managed to flutter her fan in such a frantic yet dainty manner, I had no clue. My wrists just didn't move that way.

Beverly glanced at the heavy oak trunk at our feet. "I pray we don't encounter any outlaws."

I bit back the words on the tip of my tongue. *I pray we do.*

That was the whole point of this exercise, although Beverly wasn't privy to that secret. The master plan had only been entrusted to me by our mistress, a lady of noble bearing who had to remain anonymous.

"You'll protect us, won't you, Nosey?" Beverly cooed to the oversized canine crowded into the space between our feet and the wooden chest.

I doubted it. Nosey — short for Nosewise — might look ferocious, but at heart, the Great Dane was shy as a doe. My complete opposite, in other words, in attitude *and* stature.

Nosey whined while Beverly stared out the window, on the lookout for bandits. I stared too, though for totally different reasons. Where were they already?

My breath hung in the air in anxious, frosty puffs.

"Now, ladies, don't be nervous," our driver called. "We'll protect you."

I rolled my eyes, but Beverly clasped her hands over her heart. "Thank you, Roderick."

I fingered the hilt of the sword I'd concealed. We'd be thanking that blade before we thanked creaky, nearsighted Roderick or any of the six inexperienced guards accompanying us.

A damn good thing I had a lifetime of training.

The horses' hoofbeats were muffled by the forest floor. Only the harness jangled, mingling with the sound of the occasional bird call.

"We'd better get out of here soon," Beverly fretted.

Those bandits had better get here soon, I cursed silently.

The faint trail curved ahead, affording a glimpse of the next stretch of forest. If I were a bandit, I would strike from the cover of that big oak up ahead — the one surrounded by thick foliage.

My pulse accelerated as we drew nearer, and I started an silent countdown.

Five...four...three...two...

Zing! An arrow whizzed through the air and slammed into the side of the carriage. Beverly stared stupidly as pandemonium erupted.

Dozens of cloaked men jumped out of the bushes or leaped from the trees. The horses whinnied, yanking in different directions. Roderick held on for dear life as the carriage jerked wildly, while Nosewise, Beverly, and I were thrown sideways. The guards drew their swords and swore, but that was the extent of their resistance.

"Don't move!" one of the bandits boomed in a voice an army general would envy. "Drop your weapons, and no one will be hurt."

Six swords clattered to the ground as our guards complied. So much for *Protect the treasure to the death*, as my mistress had made them swear. Then again, she'd deliberately picked the six weakest men on the roster for this duty.

But, yikes. That bandit's voice was so terrifyingly uncompromising, I nearly dropped my sword too.

"Oh Lord, oh Lord, oh Lord..." Beverly rocked in her seat.

To her credit, she did have the wherewithal to throw her lap blanket over the trunk. It didn't hide much, but the thought wasn't bad — if the idea was to hide the treasure.

I drew part of the blanket aside with my foot, and Nosey's panicked pacing did the rest.

"Whoa. Whoa there." The driver tried calming the horses.

Two bandits grabbed the harness, while the others drew their bows and aimed. Within a heartbeat, we were trapped in the center of a bristling circle of arrows.

I had to give it to them. Other than staging their ambush a tick too early, they made a fairly good impression. An impression made all the more — er, impressive — by the big, dark-haired man who strode up next, his boots crunching over cold ground.

At a distance, it was obvious he was tall. But whoa — by the time he approached, his eyes were level with the tops of the carriage windows. Huge, rounded shoulders blocked the rest of my view, and his men went silent.

"Oh Lord, oh Lord, oh Lord." Beverly rocked harder, making the little silk bows on her shoes flop back and forth.

Even I had to admit to being a teensy, tiny bit rattled. Partly by his size, but more so by his demeanor — calm and expressionless, like. . . like. . .

Like an oak tree, I decided. An oak tree with honey-colored eyes that might have been flecks of sunlight in the forest. A being that observed the world go by with no emotion whatsoever.

He clamped a hand over the carriage window, implying he could rip the door off in one quick motion.

I bit back my snarky commentary. *Okay, okay. We got the message. You're big and strong. Does intelligence also come with the package?*

Those deep eyes said, *Yes. Care to challenge me?*

I wasn't sure I did.

I fixed my eyes on his hand and winced. I'd seen a lot of scars in my time, along with raw, gory injuries. But somehow, his scars threw me off. As if I recognized them, or ought to. My eyes flitted to his face, where the impassive look changed to annoyance.

So, I have scars, Brutus might as well have growled. *You got a problem with that, lady?*

No, no problem. It was just the jarring feeling that I knew what had caused those deep, jagged gashes. I nearly said it, too — *Bear trap, huh?* — but something told me not to.

The foliage on our right rustled, and a man swung out of the trees on a vine. He let go at the last possible moment and came to a graceful landing on Beverly's side of the carriage, ending with a deep bow.

"Robert Hood, at your service."

Brutus jutted his jaw at the unnecessary theatrics, but Beverly ate it up.

"Please don't kill us, Robin Hood! Please, I beg you!"

My disguise called for me to beg and grovel too, but I just didn't have it in me. Besides, I was too busy replaying his words. Hadn't he said Robert?

I nearly corrected Beverly, but everyone knew Robin Hood was the leading bandit of Sherwood Forest. So maybe I'd heard incorrectly.

Robin Hood flashed a brilliant smile. "No need to worry, ladies. We're not here to hurt you. Just to levy a light tax."

With that, he launched into a full charm offensive, in which the smile featured prominently, along with a little innuendo and gushing praises for Beverly's beauty.

"I assure you, fair maiden, your well-being is our top priority," he murmured, fondling the tip of an arrow.

Beverly giggled. Nosewise stuck his head out the window, snuffling the man's hand.

The prince of thieves laughed and petted the dog, switching to baby talk. "Who's a good boy? Are you a good boy?"

I stared, bitterly disappointed. This was Robin Hood, the mastermind outlaw who'd made a name for himself across the country?

I glanced back to big, bad Brutus, who scooped the air with his hand. *Focus on what we came for already.*

I couldn't agree more, but Robin Hood turned to me next. "And you, fair lady..."

I crossed my arms and shot him my darkest look. The one that said, *I dare you.*

He stalled out there. "Er...um..."

"Taxes," Brutus grunted.

"Right." Robin Hood's eyes lit up at the sight of the treasure chest. "Taxes."

I nodded, tempted to chime in. *Tax time. Take it all, guys.*

That was the whole point of this mission. The state of our country was such a mess — with our dear King Richard in prison abroad and his ruthless brother, Prince John, rapidly amassing power — that my mistress deemed her treasures safer in the hands of bandits loyal to Richard than in her own castle. Times were that desperate.

This treasure must not reach Nottingham, my mistress had told me in a hurried meeting, five days earlier. *It must never fall into the hands of Prince John, who seeks to usurp his brother.*

At the time, I'd agreed wholeheartedly with the plan. But now that I'd met Robin Hood, I was doubtful. Brutus could probably be relied on to keep valuables under lock, key, and that intense gaze of his, but Robert — er, Robin? — seemed more likely to wine and dine it all away.

"Open it, John," Robin Hood ordered.

Brutus shot him a killer look that said, *No names, you moron.*

Heck, even I knew the first rule of banditry was not to be identified.

I popped open the trunk, hoping to move things along. Bows creaked and murmurs sounded as the bandits leaned in for a closer look at all that glittering treasure.

God, I hoped they remembered to keep tight hold of their arrows.

Brutus opened the carriage door — using the hinges, to my disappointment — and dragged the trunk nearer.

I pushed it along. Not that Brutus needed much help, given the bulge of his muscles.

Then he stopped suddenly, and I glanced up to find him staring.

Staring down my bodice was my first thought, and I nearly socked him.

But, no. His eyes were fixed firmly on mine, and his lips had parted in wonder. I held back my punch, at least for the moment.

What? I wanted to yell. *What?*

Brutus remained wordless, but hell. Fire zipped through my nerves, igniting my girl parts.

Nosewise stirred beside me. Beverly giggled at something Robin Hood said. But it was all muted, as if invisible forest fairies were gently guiding me to a different dimension. The place and time were the same, but everything faded into the background. All I registered was myself and Brutus.

The flecks in his eyes shone like sunshine reflecting off a river, emitting an inner fire that shouldn't have been possible.

And his mouth — not very useful in producing words, maybe, but very, very kissable, with that tempting curve that my lips would match just perfectly. Then there was that light beard outlining the triangle formed by his hard jaw and tapered chin. Unlike the bushy growths some men sported, this beard was a neat, drizzled layer that beckoned me to lean in and nuzzle him, cheek-to-cheek.

Not that I wanted to, of course. Just imagining on a purely theoretical level.

Meanwhile, Brutus didn't move. He didn't breathe. His mouth hung slightly open in a moment of recognition.

Willa, I was sure he would blurt any moment. *It's been too long.*

Much too long, I nearly agreed. But where...when...how did I know him?

His hand — the scarred one — twitched as it rested on the trunk, and I nearly reached out to touch him. But Nosewise butted between us at exactly that moment, shattering the magic spell.

Brutus dragged his eyes away from me and stared silently at the trunk.

"Need help with that, buddy?" Robin Hood chuckled.

Brutus didn't move a muscle. Our eyes met again — and again, that zing of *I know you* hit me. Then Brutus slammed the trunk lid shut, practically amputating my fingers, and shook his head.

"Not this one."

Robin Hood blinked. "What?"

Brutus went all scowly and commanding. "Not this one. This one, we let through."

Beverly clapped in relief, but Robin Hood's mouth hung ajar. So did mine, and I nearly echoed what he said next.

"What the hell?"

Beverly winced and covered her ears. I pinned Brutus with a hard look, asking the same thing.

He shoved the trunk into the middle of the carriage, making Nosewise scramble. "We're not robbing this one."

"Now, wait a minute..." Robin and several of his men protested.

I shoved the trunk back toward Brutus. "Taxes, remember?"

My murderous eyes added, *Take it, dammit.*

He pushed back, and for a minute, the trunk scraped back and forth in a reverse tug-of-war.

My cheeks heated, and I bared my teeth with effort. Finally, I leaned in, hissing, "Don't ruin this, you oaf."

Brutus blinked. "Don't...what?"

It was a whisper, but I nearly shushed him. Did he have to make a simple robbery so difficult?

"Take it. I insist," I whisper-hissed so the others wouldn't overhear.

He stared. "You want me to rob you?"

Well, not now that I was so annoyed. But my mistress had entrusted me to execute her plan, and that called for being robbed in Sherwood Forest.

He blinked stupidly. I wanted to reach out and shake him — not that I could budge that colossus, but maybe it would rattle his slow-moving mind back into action.

"Take it," I ordered.

God, I would be begging next. How could I be reduced to this?

Still, his expression remained steely.

"We're letting these ladies through — with all their possessions." He slammed the door and waved the men away. "Stand back. Hya!" He slapped the reins over a horse's hindquarters, and it shot off, dragging the others with it.

The motion threw me into the backrest of the carriage, and Beverly nearly toppled into my lap. Nosewise, too. But Beverly's door swung open, and the Great Dane leaped out in panic.

"Nosey!" Beverly and I cried at the same time.

But the horses were totally out of control, and there was no way of stopping.

"Nosey," I mourned as he disappeared into the trees.

He belonged to my mistress, but I loved that dog as much as she did. A dozen ugly scenarios popped into my mind, from Nosey tumbling into a ravine to being ripped apart by a bear.

"Poor Nosey," Beverly said, then brightened. "But thank heavens they let us go!"

I looked back, cursing. That was the burning question — why? And what gave me the bad luck to meet the only honest thieves in the forest?

My mistress's words echoed in my head. *This treasure must not reach Nottingham.*

I had never, ever failed her. Hell, I had never, ever failed, period. But right now... I held on as the carriage careened around another bend. I needed a Plan B...desperately.

Chapter Two

JOHN

The carriage careened around the next corner so fast, it nearly tipped over on two wheels. The sound of thundering hooves and a wildly jingling harness lingered a long time after the carriage raced out of sight, then faded, leaving the forest in stunned silence.

And no one more stunned than me. My heart raced, and my mind reeled from the sight of that woman.

Red hair...petite build...massive attitude...

"Um, John..." one of the guys started.

Alan wasn't so tactful. "What the hell was that about?"

I was thinking the same thing. I'd never gotten the evil eye for *not* robbing someone.

Robert shoved me. "Yeah. What the hell? We haven't seen a loot like that since...since... Well, ever."

He was right. We'd never come across a haul that rich. And I'd just granted it safe passage through Sherwood Forest.

I hung my head, telling myself it was necessary.

"Robynne said not to rob every single carriage."

A lame excuse, but I needed to get the guys off my back and my spinning mind in order.

That was her. Definitely her, my inner bear gushed, relishing the last vestiges of the woman's scent.

All around me, the guys muttered, some angry, some teasing.

"Going soft for a woman, bear?" Martin chuckled.

As if. I just wanted her out of my hair — forever. Like all females, and humans in general, she was best kept at a distance. Better yet, on a distant island.

"She wasn't even the pretty one," someone joked.

His luck that I was too shaken to slam him into the nearest tree and choke him. Had he not seen that blaze of red hair? Those green eyes? Those no-nonsense lips...

She's barely changed, my bear said dreamily.

I dug a foot into the ground, then strode off, trying to shake the memories.

I like her, my bear grumbled. *I liked her then, and I like her now.*

I shook my head. What was there to like — especially about a human?

Alan threw up his hands. "That treasure was enough for half the king's ransom."

I clenched and unclenched my right hand — the scarred one.

"Forget it," I grunted.

Which was about as likely to succeed as my forgetting the woman. How long ago had it been?

Memories stirred as I walked, blurring my surroundings. I saw the world through bear eyes, with my snout in the foreground, along with a view of a different forest. Pain pulsed through my paw, and blood oozed around the steel jaws that disappeared into fur and flesh. My fur, my flesh. The trap I'd stumbled into was buried so deep, I couldn't bring myself to look at it directly. All I could do was close my eyes and lick the wound miserably.

Humans were so clever, with such nimble fingers, they could invent anything. Yet what did they devote their efforts to? Cruel traps, like the one I'd stepped into. Thumbscrews. Iron maidens. Weapons of mass destruction.

As a shifter, not much could kill me. But a trap just might do the trick, albeit slowly.

I'd considered — then discarded — the idea of shifting into human form. The trap was powerful enough to amputate my limb entirely. So I'd lain in the damp leaves that had concealed the trap, hating humans more with every slow, agonizing minute. Had I spent an hour there? Two? Ten? I couldn't tell. Every time the blood around my wound started to crust, my tiniest, hopeful movement made the trap bite deeper, staining my fur with a fresh layer of scarlet.

The worst, though, was when footsteps sounded, and I'd spun to snarl. The sound turned to a howl of agony as the trap sank even deeper. My vision blurred, and my heart filled with rage and frustration.

I hated the world. I hated humans. I hated being helpless.

Then a woman whispered, and my ears flicked.

Oh, you poor thing...

That should have made me even angrier, because the only thing I hated more than cruelty was sympathy. But somehow, she didn't anger me. If anything, my heart beat a little slower, and the ringing noise in my ears faded.

God, I could kill those trappers... the woman had said next.

Exactly what I'd had planned — if I ever escaped that hell. Not that I had made any headway.

The woman stepped around me so quietly, I wondered if she was a fairy. She was small enough, for one thing. But, no — she was just a human. A strange one dressed in boy's clothing, with worn leather boots and a dagger at her hip. Long strands of red hair escaped her cap, shining like fire when caught by a beam of sunlight.

Not strange. She's unique, my bear mumbled. *Beautiful, too, though she seems to hide it.*

She'd crouched before me, just out of reach, studying the trap. Her scent reminded me of honey and bees — the ones that combed the sweetest flowers at the edge of the forest.

Not good, she'd murmured.

My situation wasn't, but she was. Good, I mean. Somehow, I could sense it.

Which only went to show how delirious the pain made me, because there were no good humans.

Perhaps she really was a forest fairy, because she convinced me — and herself — that it was okay to edge closer, slip her dagger between the jaws of the trap, and prepare to lever.

This is going to hurt, she'd whispered, *but it will make you free. Just please, please don't kill me.*

I didn't, and I doubt I could have. I was too busy writhing in agony as she levered the trap in an excruciatingly long process. Finally, it sprung open, causing as much damage as it had on the way in. But I was free, if shaking and panting. By the time I'd opened my eyes, she'd leaped away.

You're free, she whispered sadly. Her tone implied I was unlikely to survive, but at least I would have my dignity.

"Watch it, man," Alan grumbled, dragging me back to the present.

I'd just let a branch swat him in the face. Oops. Sorry. Not sorry?

I blinked at the trees, then the surrounding forest. Sherwood Forest in winter, not that other place in spring a decade earlier.

I clenched and unclenched my hand. Since I was a shifter, my wounds had healed enough to leave me with some range of motion. Not enough to grasp a spoon, maybe, but enough to grip the long, thick staff I used as a weapon. A weapon I thumped along the ground now, warning the other men to keep their distance.

"John, man," Alan tut-tutted. "How are you ever going to explain this to Robynne?"

I shrugged. I could barely explain it to myself. How could I explain to Robynne?

By the time I trudged into camp, I'd gone from confusion to frustration. I hated being in debt to anyone — least of all, a human. Now, I'd finally evened a score that had hung over me for years. So, why wasn't I relieved? Why didn't it feel like closure but rather, the dawn of a whole new problem?

"You're not going to believe this, Robynne," Robert called to his sister.

I sighed, tempted to drown my sorrows in my secret stash of honey. But home-brewed ale was a closer option, so I filled the tin cup we shared, downed it in one, and thumped the cup back onto the barrel.

Robynne — *the* Robynne of Hood fame, though no one outside our little band knew she was a woman — raised a single eyebrow as Robert and the others filled her in on what had happened. Then the dogs went wild barking when a deer barreled into camp. No, wait — a dog. A really big one.

"Nosewise!" Robert patted his thighs, calling his new friend over.

Robynne shushed the barking dogs and studied the Great Dane, then her brother. "You stole a dog from a fancy lord or lady?"

Robert interrupted his *Who'sagoodboy* doggie talk long enough to answer her. "No. We had the loot of the year in our hands, and John Littlebrain let it slip through our fingers."

"Actually, he handed it right back to them," Alan added, still sour.

Old, toothless Christopher murmured one of those cryptic, pseudo-wise comments he specialized in. "Like they say, wealth comes and goes like a goose in spring."

I glared at everyone, then folded my arms and gazed at our fearless leader, waiting.

Yes, our fearless leader, a woman. Originally, the men had appointed me their leader, but that was before Robynne had come along. Within a week, we'd voted unanimously for her to take over.

Why? For the same reason the Great Dane sat still as a statue at Robynne's firm command. Robynne was a born leader. She was smarter than any of us — and fairer. Tougher in some ways, gentler in others. Deadly with a sword and downright lethal with her bow and every perfectly aimed arrow. Under Robynne, our camp had gone from a ramshackle hovel to an orderly, livable hamlet. And we men had gone from wanton robbers to crusaders with a higher cause.

All in all, Robynne was a better leader than I would ever be. I was man enough to recognize that — and frankly, relieved to drop to second-in-command. I liked my life simple. Uncomplicated. Low on drama.

Which was why I shouldn't be so fixated on the redhead with the striking green eyes from the carriage. As a woman and a human, she was a simmering recipe for *complication* and *drama.*

And yet, I couldn't help thinking of her. Dreaming of her. Glancing in the direction she'd disappeared and wondering if I'd lost my chance forever.

I frowned, sniffing the wind. My chance at what?

Robynne glanced in the same direction, then tilted her head. Everyone went dead silent, awaiting her judgment. Even the dogs looked up, drooling in reverent silence.

"The loot of the year, you say?" Robynne mused. "Well, that's the tricky thing about treasure. Figuring out what's worth keeping and what's better to let go of."

Robert scratched his head, trying to puzzle out a hidden meaning. He would be puzzling for a while, because all the brains of the family had gone to Robynne.

Most of the men looked as confused as Robert, but nobody dared speak. As for me, I stared at Robynne, wondering if she knew about me and the woman in the carriage. But, no. Robynne's gaze had gone distant, almost wistful.

She did that sometimes. As if her body remained in Sherwood Forest but her heart was elsewhere. I could guess at the reason, though I would never, ever tell anyone. Robynne's secrets were hers, and like the rest of her, definitely not to be messed with.

"Figuring out the true treasure is the tricky part," she whispered quietly. "And realizing that before it's too late."

Chapter Three

WILLA

"Thank goodness we got through." Beverly crossed herself as the carriage rattled into Nottingham. "Thank goodness."

I scowled, still cursing that oaf in the forest. What kind of bandit let a perfectly willing victim go?

"Thanks to that dimwit," I muttered. When Beverly glanced over, I spoke louder. "I mean, that angel of mercy."

The horses' hoofbeats became a muted thump over the wood of a drawbridge, then a sharp clang over cobblestones. We were entering Nottingham — with the treasure, dammit!

For the hundredth time, I cursed the honest thief who'd refused to rob us. The giant of a man with a misplaced sense of chivalry and... and...

I was ready to add a string of expletives, but my mind sidetracked to other things, like all that hard muscle. The beard that looked so soft and supple. And most of all, those warm, honest eyes. Eyes I was sure I'd seen before. But where? And why did I yearn to see them again?

Oaf, oaf, oaf, I reminded myself.

Plus, he probably had a secondary motive, as my mother had constantly warned about men. Having been in love once, widowed twice, and cheated on by the third and last of her common-law husbands, she'd raised my sisters and me with a clear agenda. As women, we had to be resourceful, quick-witted, and above all, fiercely independent. We couldn't count on men to defend or provide for us. If a man treated us well, it was best to be suspicious, because men had ulterior motives. Sex topped the list, followed by other desires, like being served day in, day out by a good cook and a handy, live-in housekeeper.

As for the oaf, he was sure to demand I repay his "favor" if we ever crossed paths again. Well, I knew better than to fall for such treachery.

The carriage plunged into shadow as we passed under the city gate, then lurched into daylight as we emerged on the market square. The driver pulled his team to a halt, and Beverly uttered her hundredth *Thank goodness.*

The carriage was our mistress's finest — part of the bait for those idiot thieves in the forest — making heads swivel. Even the poor wretch shackled to the town stocks looked up at the commotion. But when Beverly alit and started jabbering about our ordeal, no one looked particularly impressed.

"We were nearly robbed!" she cried over and over.

A man shrugged. "Happens every week, lady. The only thing that makes you special is you got through."

I frowned from my vantage point in the carriage. The thing was, we didn't *get* through. We were *permitted* through. Why?

"Aren't you going to do something about it?" Beverly admonished the guard.

"Well, seeing as you weren't actually robbed..." he reasoned.

"But...but..." Beverly sputtered.

Another guard yawned. "If you want, you can report it to the sheriff." He didn't actually say, *He probably cares less than I do,* but that was clear from his expression.

Beverly snapped her fingers. "Well then, fetch him."

I nearly jumped out of the carriage to shush her, but I was too late. Over the past decade, the sheriff of Nottingham had made a name for himself through cruelty, torture, and extortion. Worse, he was an ally of that usurper, Prince John.

I glanced at the trunk at my feet as my mistress's orders echoed through my mind. *This treasure must not reach Nottingham. It must not fall into the hands of Prince John.*

But, crap. Here it was, right in that den of lions.

My mind spun. Could I grab the reins, gallop back to the forest, and force the outlaws to take the treasure? Tempting, but a little farfetched.

Could I hide it? Good idea, except we were in the middle of an open square, surrounded by guards. Not exactly a lot of concealment options.

"What crime would I report to the sheriff?" the second guard protested.

"Well, they stole our dog," Beverly tried.

Not really, but the argument bought me some time. If only it brought me some brilliant brain waves too.

My eye caught on Beverly — or rather, the jewelry that weighed her down. Our mistress had insisted Beverly wear several stunning pieces, making her a display case the outlaws of Sherwood Forest couldn't ignore.

If only the outlaws we'd been counting on weren't so stupid — or so damned honest.

A stunning sapphire-and-ruby necklace graced Beverly's delicate frame, and a diamond-studded tiara crowned her elaborate hairdo. But the item that shone the brightest when the sun peered out between clouds was the plain ring around her finger. It only shone for a moment, but I imagined it calling out, *Don't leave me!*

Then the sun ducked back behind clouds, and the shine faded like a coin plunging down a long, dark well.

I blinked, dismissing the distraction. It was time to cut my losses and salvage anything I could.

Moving quickly, I closed the carriage curtains, opened the trunk, and raked my fingers through the contents. I couldn't make off with everything, but I could slip away with the most valuable items. The question was, which?

The most obvious are not always the most valuable, my mistress had said when she'd packed the trunk. *On the surface, some are more modest, but those are often the ones spelled with ancient magic.*

Magic? I riffled through coins, rings, and gems. Now, as then, I was dubious. But who was I to distrust the wisdom of my mistress?

"All right, all right. We'll fetch the sheriff," one of the guards grumbled outside.

I studied the treasures. What to take and what to abandon?

One obvious choice was the dagger near the top. My mistress claimed it was spelled, but mostly, I chose it for its thin, glinting blade. The rest was harder to decide on. With time running out, I couldn't be choosy, so I went for practical. I threw on as many necklaces as I could and squeezed a dozen rings onto my fingers. In a pinch, they could double as brass knuckles.

"Willa," Beverly called. "Come now. We must prepare to greet the sheriff."

Greet a cruel monster? No thank you. I threw on another diamond necklace, tucked it out of sight, then pushed aside a gold cross the size of a shovel.

"Willa," Beverly urged. "He's coming. Hurry!"

"I am," I said truthfully, though for an entirely different purpose.

A peek through the curtains showed a tall, handsome man striding toward the carriage. *Really* tall and *really* handsome, like a knight straight out of legend. People scurried out of his way, though he didn't seem in a hurry. In fact, he stopped to pick up the basket a woman dropped while juggling a bag and a baby. He handed over the basket with a polite word and ruffled the child's hair before continuing.

Clearly, Nottingham had a few kind souls to balance out that awful sheriff.

Then I spotted the heavy collar hung loosely over his shoulders — the mark of the sheriff's office. Wait. *That* was the sheriff?

Well, men could be tricky that way. My mother had taught me all about that. So, I had to hurry.

Loosening the strings of my bodice, I stuffed in as many items as I could fit. Which was quite a bit, given my small size and the space that dress could expand to. Finally, I threw a pouch of coins and two Holy Grail look-alikes into my bag. I would have loved to take that bejeweled sword, but that would be too obvious. Then I threw on my cloak and eased the far door open. Most of the guards were with Beverly on the other side of the carriage, but I was still in plain view of two others. I slid to the ground, praying the coins wouldn't clink.

One of the guards eyeballed me. "And where are you off to, missy?"

I grimaced and held my stomach. "Cramps. It's that time of the month. Where's the nearest privy?"

He grimaced as if I had brought up witchcraft rather than a natural monthly occurrence, then pointed to an alley. "Down there."

I was three steps away when he called out sharply. "Wait!"

Ice slid down my spine, and I turned slowly.

"Yes?"

I prepared to drop the loot, draw my dagger, and fight my way out of there.

He motioned to my bag. "What's in there?"

Ha. I had him now. "Girl things." I clutched it to my chest. "You know, for—"

He waved me away before I could get into any gory details. "All right, already. Go. But make sure you're back quickly. The sheriff may want to question you."

I sprint-walked away, keeping the bag close to my body. So fast, I barely had time to glance at the wanted posters.

Wanted: Robin Hood, for ten counts of banditry...

I rolled my eyes. If only today had been number eleven...

The latrine was all the way at the end of an alley, in a corner of the city walls that smelled god-awful. I bypassed it and turned the corner, cursing myself for taking too much. There was no way I could move swiftly with so much clanking treasure.

Use your head, Willa, I could practically hear my mother say.

I looked around as I ran. Halfway up the next stretch of alley, I ducked into a shed crisscrossed with spider webs. Inside, I stripped my outer layers, then practically ripped off the frilly collar and corset. I bounced on one foot, changing into the clothes in my bag. My regular clothes, thank goodness.

The scandalous ones, because what woman wore pants and a goatherd's jacket?

If someone had stopped to ask me, I would have given them my usual answer: *It's my jacket, and I'll wear whatever I want, dammit.*

I'd grown up lucky that way. My mother was too busy toiling her way up from *destitute* to building a profitable wool-trading business to make much fuss about her tomboy daughter, so my attire and attitude went largely unchecked.

That's just Willa, my mother would sigh at the neighbors' admonitions. *You can no more tame her than you can tame a deer in the wild.*

Another plus was that my mother insisted her daughters learn how to defend themselves, using a variety of tutors — usually men who owed her money. Generally, my mother didn't believe in borrowing or lending, but she did make strategic exceptions for local tradesmen whose indebtedness might pay off in other ways. I'd done stints with an aging knight, a cooper who'd once served as a yeoman archer, and a blacksmith with a penchant for sparring with battle-axes. Thus, I'd learned to fight with a variety of weapons — and my bare hands, if necessary.

But I couldn't take on every guard in Nottingham, so I had to think of another solution to my immediate problem. That meant bundling the loot inside my dress, then climbing into the rafters. Balancing precariously, I wedged the bundle into a dim corner. That would have to do until I could come back and retrieve it — along with the rest of the treasure, Lord willing.

Shouts broke out in the distance, hurrying me along. Apparently, my absence had been noticed.

"Where did she go?" someone roared.

"She's made off with part of the treasure!" another man hollered.

I exited swiftly. The voices were still around the corner, but they were approaching quickly.

"Hurry! She can't have gotten far."

I rolled my eyes. If that was the portly guard I'd spoken to, I could cover twice the distance he was capable of and twice as swiftly.

"We're looking for a lady. Green dress, red hair. Very red hair," someone shouted.

I ran, tucking my hair into a cap, and hung my dagger loosely at my waist. I only slowed at the next corner, in sight of the west gate. If I stooped a little and kept my bag slung over my shoulder, I could pass for a man — or at least a boy.

Indeed, I did, as I joined the line of people going about their business in and out of the city. The guards were too busy warming their hands over a fire to give me a second glance, and minutes later, I was outside the city walls.

I did my best to maintain a casual pace for the first half mile. Then, after a quick glance around, I cut across the dead, frosty fields, heading straight for Sherwood Forest. A mile later, I crouched to touch the bubbling surface of the river that formed a boundary between the tamed and wild worlds. Behind me were the farms, fields, and hedgerows. Ahead lay a deep, dark forest — the realm of wolves, bears, and outlaws.

A few years ago, I might have rushed in just for the adventure. Now, I knew better.

I looked back toward Nottingham. If things had gone according to plan, I would be safe and secure in the city, where no one would question my story about being robbed. My mistress's treasure would be safely hidden from Prince John, my mission completed.

Instead, the treasure was in enemy hands, and I had to procure something I hated: assistance.

I peered into the forest. My mistress had been adamant that the treasure go to the outlaws in Sherwood Forest, so I would have to start there.

The question was, could I shake some sense into those stupid outlaws, or would I die trying? What if there was more than one band of outlaws? A smarter one, maybe?

I could only hope.

Either way, the answer lay in the forest.

I jumped from boulder to boulder to cross the river, then took a deep breath and entered the dim, dangerous world of Sherwood Forest.

Chapter Four

JOHN

Hours after the *Robbery That Wasn't*, as Robert bitterly called it, I took off to stomp grumpily through the woods. Alone, because half the guys were still furious/frustrated/incredulous, and the other half drove me crazy by cheerily pretending nothing had happened. Robynne didn't mind about the treasure, but she had been pinning me with piercing, *I'm trying to figure you out* looks I was desperate to evade.

So, off I went, thrashing through the undergrowth like a clueless human — or a grouchy bear — trying to get the fiery redhead with emerald eyes out of my mind.

Yet everywhere I went, she stuck with me.

I grunted, kicking the ground. What right did she have to cling so tenaciously to my mind?

Tenacious... my bear murmured approvingly.

I tried focusing on berries... honey... nuts... Anything to distract myself.

Even then, she haunted my mind. I saw her in the distant past, murmuring softly to my pathetic, trapped bear. I saw her in a vision from that very morning, eyes ablaze and cheeks flushed. I saw the two of us locked in a heated kiss somewhere I couldn't place. A kiss that hadn't happened...

Yet, my bear murmured dreamily.

I stomped deeper into the woods. Overhead, an owl hooted and blinked saucer-size eyes. A deer froze, then bounded away. Smaller forest-dwellers scurried away at my approach too — voles, squirrels, and pine martens scratching for some sustenance in the depths of winter. Each might as well have muttered, *What the hell happened to ruin your day?*

She happened, I growled.

The more I walked, the worse it became.

Take it. I insist, she'd said that morning in the carriage.

My bear licked its lips, giving the words a whole new twist.

And, *zoom!* Off went my fantasies, changing the setting to a candlelit bedroom and tweaking her words to make that, *Take me.*

My groin ached at the vision of red hair fanned out over a pillow and green eyes smoldering at me — in a good way. Quick, capable hands touching me...

You're a thief, right? So, rob me, already.

I groaned. Maybe I'd spent a little too much time alone in the woods. Maybe the guys were right about finding some female shifters to share camp with. Ideally, sex-craving, relationship-averse females — if such a thing was even possible.

At the sound of rushing water, I picked up my pace. That was what I needed — some time on my favorite rock beside the babbling brook that zigzagged merrily through the forest.

The banks were rocky enough to create a clearing, and when I stepped out, I practically sighed in relief. For a moment, the woman was gone, replaced by the simple pleasure of sunshine on my face. After several gray, dreary days, this was just what I needed. I sat on a rock and shut my eyes, listening to gurgling water.

I was just getting into a relaxed state — slow breaths, mind filled with images of cranberries and honey — when a bird exploded out of a nearby tree. I snapped my eyes open and reached for my quarterstaff. Something — or someone — was approaching.

A human, I realized. Great. Yet another uninvited visitor to my forest.

But unlike the noisy carriage from earlier, this person was on foot and very, very stealthy. Either he was an incredibly skilled woodsman, or I was losing my touch. Normally, my keen bear senses could sense someone approaching from a hundred yards away. This man was as close as twenty or thirty paces.

Or rather, this young lad, judging by his slight size. Which only annoyed me more.

I stood, gripping my staff tightly. An intruder was an intruder, and I would send him packing.

The lad's step hitched when he noticed me, but he didn't stop until he was on the opposite side of the brook. There, he planted his feet and waited.

I frowned. Had he no clue about the ways of the forest? I tested the air for his scent, but the breeze was coming from the wrong direction.

"Your name, boy." My voice boomed over the sound of rushing water.

His was a squeak. "Will Scarlet. And you?"

Lord, his voice hadn't even broken. What was this kid doing wandering through the woods?

"John Little," I barked. "And what exactly are you after?"

"Not looking for trouble. Just looking to be on my way."

"Well, your way isn't through Sherwood Forest." I planted my staff, giving him one last chance to turn tail and run.

"Ah, but it is. Don't mind me, though." With that, he moved toward the large, flat stepping-stones that crossed the brook.

I turned my staff sideways and growled. "No, you don't."

He looked up, giving me a glimpse of thin, almost feminine features. Then he tugged his hood lower and made an impatient gesture. "Fine, you cross first."

I squared my shoulders, waiting. Then I frowned and prompted him. "Aren't you going to challenge me?"

"For the right to cross the river first? God, no. You go ahead. But make it quick. It's too cold to dally."

My brow furrowed. Apparently, this lad was too young to know the rules. Okay, those rules were unspoken, but every man knew it was critical to establish dominance from the first moment of an encounter. And in an encounter like this, both parties were supposed to glare and make a show of slowly drawing weapons, then lazily examining the blades of their swords or the fletching of their arrows to make an even bigger impression.

But this guy did neither. He just gestured impatiently. "Go on, already. Cross." When I didn't move, he threw up his hands. "Don't be ridiculous."

My frown deepened. It wasn't ridiculous. It was a time-honored way of establishing masculine hierarchy. And I always, always came out at the top of the pyramid.

Maybe he doesn't know, my bear said. *Maybe he's not from around here.*

Well, that much was obvious. I changed tacks. "There's a tax for crossing, and you have to pay."

He rolled his eyes. "There's no bloody tax in the forest. There are no rules. That's the whole purpose of entering lawless country."

A good point, not that I was about to admit it.

"Pay up, you rascal, or I'll chase you all the way back to Nottingham."

When he laughed — *laughed!* — his voice cracked. "I don't have any money."

My temper rose. Money wasn't the issue. Respect was, and it was about time he showed some.

I leaped onto the first of the stepping-stones and brandished my staff. "You can come on out here and get the whipping you've been begging for, boy, or you can show some sense and run back to wherever you came from."

When he stuck his hands on his hips, I nearly laughed, because that *really* made him appear feminine.

"That's ridiculous," he complained. "You'd beat me in an instant."

I flashed a toothy grin, hinting at the beast inside me. "Actually, I was planning on drawing it out, just for fun."

Instead of cringing, the lad just turned up the attitude.

"Your idea of fun is beating on someone half your size? That's hardly fair."

"Life isn't fair, boy. But I will show you mercy and fight you on the log if you prefer." I pointed to the right, where a log made a bridge over a deeper section of water.

He considered for a moment, then reached for his dagger.

I shook my head. "My forest, my choice of weapon. We fight with quarterstaffs."

Another eye roll. This boy reminded me of my sister.

"What if I don't have one?"

I grinned, because I had an answer to that. "I'll make you one. Wait here."

As I jumped back to the riverbank, my mood lifted for the first time in hours. Finally, I had that infernal woman out of my head — and an amusing little challenge.

"You're kidding," the boy muttered when I found a suitable branch and started trimming. "You'd rather make a staff and fight me than just cross the river?"

No, I wasn't kidding. Not that I graced him with an answer.

The bushes on my side of the brook rustled, and Robynne emerged. "What's going on?"

I motioned impatiently. "Will Scarlet here thinks Sherwood Forest is his playground. I'm about to teach him a lesson."

Robynne studied the intruder, then tilted her head. "Will Scarlet, you say?"

She put all the emphasis on the first name, as if she thought it ought to be something else. Then she flashed a sly smile, murmuring, "Interesting. Very interesting."

I huffed. The lad wasn't interesting. He was annoying — almost as annoying as that redhead in the carriage.

"And what exactly do you seek in Sherwood Forest, Will?" Robynne called.

Trouble, I nearly grumbled.

The boy let a beat go by before answering. "I'm looking for Robin Hood."

Robynne barely hid her amusement. "And what is your business with Robin Hood?"

"I'll tell him when I find him," the boy retorted.

I shot Robynne a sour look as I spoke into her mind. *See? He's impertinent. Annoying. Disrespectful.*

A smile played over Robynne's lips, but she ignored me.

"So, the plan is...?" she asked the boy.

"To earn the right to enter the forest by fighting me," I interjected.

The boy sighed. "On a log. With quarterstaffs. So logical."

Robynne chuckled. "Well, I'd hate to interrupt such an important, manly ritual. I'll just watch from here."

With that, she plopped down on a sunny rock, looking more amused than I'd ever seen our fearless leader.

I motioned Will to the log and tossed him my staff, keeping the new one.

"Look. I'm even giving you the better weapon."

"Such a gentleman," he muttered.

"Come on, then." I stepped out onto the log.

The minute I did, second thoughts hit. That log wasn't as wide as it looked — and it was slippery. I would have to make this quick and painless.

The boy glanced down at the rushing water. "I hope you can swim."

I couldn't, but he didn't need to know that. Besides, I wouldn't be the one falling.

"Just get out here," I snipped.

"This, I have to see," Robynne chuckled behind me.

The boy took a first dainty step onto the log. Yes, dainty. If I hadn't had such a crappy morning, I might have taught him about instilling fear in your opponent.

Holding my staff in both hands, I stepped forward, claiming the widest part of the log before he did. I angled my staff to one side, then the other to confuse him. Then I shot my top hand forward, slamming my staff against his.

It was only a testing blow, but the boy staggered. I grinned. This would all be over within a few seconds.

Then I launched my real attack, a sequence of six blows. Six in theory, that is. Most men didn't make it past blow number two, and none had ever lasted past four. Staff fighting was an underappreciated art form, so I rarely got to enjoy a good fight.

But somehow, Will dodged or deflected his way all the way through position number six. Then he stood, panting, warily awaiting my next attack.

I blinked. Next attack? How was that possible?

Robynne chuckled in my mind. *John Little, meet your match.*

I growled. This little pipsqueak was not my match. He'd simply avoided most of my blows. I'd have him off the log in no time.

I lashed out with a different sequence — one of only four moves, each brutally effective.

Triumph washed over me when the second move threw him off-balance, and the third finished him off. One moment, he was windmilling his arms, desperately trying to salvage a hopeless situation, and the next, he dropped like a stone.

"Ha!" I hooted, watching him go.

At least, I started to. But the little weasel grabbed my staff, and a moment later, I was falling too. Falling...falling...

Splash! Just before hitting the water, I heard Robynne's roar of laughter. Then I went under, gasping as icy water rushed into my ears, nose, and mouth. Losing all sense of which way was up, I crashed into Will, and our arms and legs tangled.

In staff fighting, I was a champion. In swimming...not exactly. In truth, I avoided deep water — defined by anything deeper than my shins, or better yet, my ankles.

Yet there I was, completely submerged in icy, swirling water.

Will shoved me away, as if the fall was my fault. As we grappled in a race to the surface, my hand contacted something soft and plump. Something that made no sense, but all I could think of at that moment was survival.

When I finally made it to the surface, eerie, underwater sounds were replaced by the chuckle of my opponent, which really ticked me off. Then I went down a second time. Torrents of water spun me around, tangling me in my cloak. Bit by bit, my waterlogged clothing dragged me deeper. By then, the cold had practically stopped my heart, and I was fading.

I cursed the depth...the powerful current...and mostly, myself.

When the fabric around my neck tightened, I thought my cloak had wrapped around something and this was the end.

But I was jerked upward, and a moment later, I broke through the surface.

Someone yelled in my ear, but I couldn't hear above my own coughs and gasps. Whoever it was — Will? — twisted their wrist, keeping a firm grip on me.

God, did I hate being helpless.

Eventually, I made out what he was muttering.

"You can't swim?"

Wasn't that obvious?

"What idiot agrees to fight over water when he can't swim — in winter?" he complained.

Me, I supposed.

"Oh, for goodness' sake..." he muttered — bitterly, like he was the one who'd nearly drowned.

Then it hit me. The high voice. The body I'd made contact with...

My nose and mouth were barely above the waterline, but I twisted to stare at my adversary. The water had swept away his cap, revealing long red hair and a willowy figure.

"You're a woman?" I sputtered.

"And you're an idiot," she muttered.

I started going under a third time, but she yanked me up. "Oh no, you don't."

Like I'd done it on purpose or something.

"I'll tow you," she went on in that same annoyed tone. "Just stop flailing!"

"I'm swimming," I said between watery coughs.

"You're flailing, and it doesn't help."

"I don't need help!"

"Fine. Swim on your own, then."

I did my best but only succeeded in moving frigid water, rather than my body.

"I said swim, not splash," she complained. "Just reach and paddle. Like this."

She demonstrated with a smooth, effortless stroke — as if my panicked mind had room to process anything.

I went under for the third time. The last time? My clothes pulled me down, and ice clogged my bloodstream.

Then my collar tightened again, and I was back on the surface, where the woman was still chewing me out.

"—you useless oaf." I'd missed the first part of her rant, but I got the gist. "Just keep still. We're nearly there."

We weren't nearly there. We were miles away from the bank.

Okay, okay — the brook was only a few yards across, but it might as well have been miles.

She was angry and bitter, but tenacious as hell in towing me. Not long after, my hand struck the shore. Finally, I got my feet under me — weakly — and glared.

"You're a woman."

She rolled her eyes. "It's a gender, not a disease."

Somewhere up on the riverbank, Robynne chuckled.

"You said Will," I growled through chattering teeth.

She shrugged. "It's Willa. Close enough?"

A long, drippy standoff ensued, in which Willa refused to stand down. I didn't either, mainly because any movement risked me falling back into the water.

"Need a hand?" Robynne grinned at me from the steep embankment.

Willa scowled. "Oh, he doesn't need help. Can't you tell?"

I ignored them both, grateful the guys weren't there. I would never live this down.

With Robynne pulling and Willa pushing — not at all gently, I might point out — I hauled myself up the bank and lay there like a dying fish. Willa jumped from foot to foot, trying to warm up. I cursed her for a dozen things, including seizing a height advantage.

Temporary height advantage, I reminded myself.

My bear hummed dreamily. *She's beautiful. Like a mermaid.*

A surly mermaid, I muttered back.

My bear shook its head. *Beautiful. One of a kind.*

Okay, so the beast had a point. With her long hair slicked back and waterdrops sliding slowly down her face, she looked the part. Her wet clothes stuck to her, revealing feminine curves. Her green eyes were bright and confident, like a creature who ruled her watery world. . .

Yes, the mermaid image certainly worked — until she gathered her cloak in both hands and wrung it out over my head.

I was already freezing, but I swear, those drops came straight from the Arctic. Closing my eyes, I prayed for Robynne to end my misery and chase this unwanted female out of our turf. Neither humans nor mermaids had a place in our forest.

But a moment later, I groaned, because when Robynne spoke. . .

"Good to meet you, Willa. You said you're looking for Robin Hood?"

Another careful nod.

Robynne grinned and delivered the punch line. "Well, you found me. I'm Robynne. Robynne Hood."

I eked a little satisfaction from the stunned silence that ensued.

"Nice to meet you," Willa finally peeped.

Robynne gave Willa a respectful pat on the shoulder.

"Welcome to Sherwood Forest." Then she tilted her head. "Let me guess. You're the one from the carriage this morning."

Willa nodded warily.

"And you're back now," Robynne mused.

Huh. A damned good point. What the hell was this woman after? Or was her purpose on earth simply to torture me?

Willa gave another guarded nod.

"Interesting. Very interesting," Robynne murmured.

It wasn't interesting. It was suspicious as hell. But I was too busy coughing up water to point that out.

Robynne's eyes sparkled, and she flashed a mischievous smile. "Well then, Willa. Can I invite you to our camp?"

I groaned. This was not happening.

Willa glanced back at me. "What about him?"

Her words didn't have a sliver of warmth, but apparently, now that she'd saved my life — for the second time, dammit — she felt responsible for me.

Great. Just great.

"You're okay, aren't you, John?" Robynne called cheerily.

"Fine," I growled.

Inside, I cursed fate for allowing me to repay my debt to Willa that morning, only to turn around and make me owe her again.

"See? He's fine," Robynne said breezily. Then her voice dropped to that conspiratorial tone women used with others of their tribe. "But you and I need to talk."

Chapter Five

WILLA

The following hour was the coldest — and most surreal — of my life. I was following Robynne Hood, master outlaw, through Sherwood Forest. *The* Robynne Hood — a living legend whose notoriety had spread like wildfire, though the facts had gotten twisted along the way. Like the fact that she was a woman.

"Typical," I muttered. "Women never get the credit they deserve."

"True," Robynne agreed from a few steps ahead. "But that can also come in handy at times."

I supposed so, though it still pained me.

She'd loaned me her cloak, and I tugged it close to my body, distracting myself from the cold.

"Who is Robert?" I asked, trying to puzzle it all out.

"My brother." Robynne's sigh painted a detailed image of a foolhardy younger sibling she'd always had to bail out from his own follies. Then she turned back to call, "John? You still with us?"

A grumble was his only reply.

The big, wet, surly man had kept his distance ever since we'd left the brook. I studiously ignored him. At least, I tried. But someone that big — and that much of a mystery — commanded a large corner of my mind.

Where did he get those scars? Why did I feel I knew him? And would his beard prove as soft as it looked if I reached out to nuzzle it?

I gave myself a shake, focusing on the woods instead. I'd given up on memorizing the way a while ago — the trail meandered too much, with too many forks to remember, so I was truly at Robynne's mercy. Still, I didn't feel any threat, just a foreboding sense of events spinning out of my control.

I threw another sour look behind me, though the woods were silent. For such a big guy, John sure moved soundlessly. Robynne did too, barely making the undergrowth stir despite her no-time-to-waste pace. Clearly, this was a woman who got things done.

I liked her already. The question was, could I trust her?

As the trail wound onward, pines and yews gave way to towering oaks with mighty branches that seemed to support the forest canopy and even the sky above it. Pockets of snow clung to tree trunks and hollows, and periodically, an owl hooted, keeping a lookout.

Who, who? it asked. *Who are you?*

I peered around. Wait. Was that an owl or a good imitation?

I whirled at a sound to my left, convinced we were being followed. Robynne didn't seem concerned, so it must have been her own forces.

Eventually, we crested a rise, and Robynne called out, loud and clear.

"Hello, hello. Robynne and John are back, and we've brought a visitor."

Clearly a warning. I pursed my lips, wondering what her men might scurry to hide. Looted treasure? Stolen weapons? Drying underwear?

Whatever it was, they went about it silently, and when we came to a clearing a short time later, twenty men waited silently.

"Hello, everyone," Robynne said. "This is Willa. Willa Scarlet."

I made myself as tall as I could. Which wasn't very tall, but hey. It was all in the attitude.

A few doffed their hats, while others looked me over. No leering, thank goodness — the plus side of falling in with a group of bandits led by a woman.

I couldn't help staring around in wonder. Not at the men, who were pretty much what I'd expected — not hardened criminals so much as farmers, shepherds, or simple townsfolk eking out a new life after fleeing harsh sentences for petty crimes. What was our country coming to?

"Wow. Nice camp," I couldn't help murmuring.

Shelters dotted the area, many built into trees with second and even third stories extending into overhead branches, tree-house-style. A stream ran through the middle of the camp, with little channels diverting to each hut, providing running water.

The dwellings surrounded a gnarled, ancient oak with roots protruding high enough to serve as benches. Posts supported a roof, creating an open-sided meeting area, complete with a fire pit for roasting meat or hosting bonfires.

In towns, people pushed nature away. Here, they lived with nature, intertwined.

It was easy to imagine music, a crackling fire, and roars of laughter as a small community celebrated important occasions — the changing of the seasons, perhaps, or a warm, dry spell. A birthday, a successful hunt...

I gulped. Or a successful robbery. Not that they'd had one today. But I wasn't to blame for that. That was all on John.

He held his head high as he emerged from the woods, but his knuckles were tight around his staff. I almost felt sorry for him.

Almost. He was the one who'd ruined everything, right?

Still, my heart gave a little pang. Thrashing around underwater was not my idea of fun, but that moment of contact when we'd first fallen in gave me an inexplicable zing. His arms had grabbed mine, and when our torsos brushed...

A deep, booming bark broke out, and a huge body launched itself at me. I staggered backward, then cried out. "Nosewise!"

He snuffled and licked me, beside himself with excitement.

"Nosey," I murmured, hugging him.

For a moment, I closed my eyes, thinking of home. Wishing myself there, almost. But when I remembered my unfinished mission, I straightened, shushing Nosey.

"You're one of those ladies from the carriage," one of the men said, a little dumbfounded. Robert, the handsome, dim-witted brother, I realized.

Another man scratched his head. "Doesn't look like a fine lady now."

"So..." Robert rubbed his jaw. "You didn't get robbed this morning, and now you're back because...?"

Everyone peered at me, including Robynne, whose eyes posed the same question.

I pursed my lips, trying to decide how much to reveal.

"Because she wanted it stolen," Robynne surmised after the silence stretched awkwardly.

My breath caught. Well, yes. But now that she said it aloud...

"That's ridiculous," one of the men guffawed. "Who wants to be robbed?"

Robynne tapped her foot, thinking. "A good question."

"Someone who doesn't want what they have?" Robert tried.

Another man frowned. "Maybe the loot is cursed, and she was trying to skive it off on us."

Not the craziest suggestion, I supposed, though it was way off.

Finally, I fessed up, figuring that was the best way to salvage my mission. "It's not cursed. And yes, I wanted you to take it. Well, my mistress did."

"And who exactly is your mistress?" John demanded, still gripping his staff tightly. Strangling it instead of me, perhaps?

"A noble lady who wishes to remain anonymous. One loyal to King Richard..." I paused, gauging their reaction.

Several men raised fists, and others crossed their hearts solemnly. "The one true king. Not that usurping brother of his."

"Prince John isn't even trying to raise the king's ransom," another man grumbled. "Those taxes he keeps raising are for his own benefit."

So, whew. We'd guessed correctly about these bandits' allegiance.

"My mistress is a woman of great wealth and standing. She feared Prince John would confiscate her valuables for his own profit instead of using them to pay the king's ransom. She tasked me with bringing her greatest treasures here, where they would be safe." I glared around, challenging them. "Was she wrong?"

To a man, they shook their heads and swore allegiance to the king.

"Not a bad plan," Robynne admitted. "In fact, we've been saving up for the ransom ourselves."

"It was a *great* plan." I didn't add, *Except he ruined it,* but I did shoot a slitty-eyed look at John.

He stuck up his hands. "I didn't know!"

"You didn't listen," I hissed. "Men never listen."

Half the guys looked at the ground, while the other half looked at Robynne.

She and I exchanged knowing looks, and she sighed. "I get it. Believe me, I get it."

"Fine. We'll just steal some other treasure," John tried.

"It has to be this one," I said.

"Why this particular loot?"

I hesitated just long enough for John to point an accusing finger. "See? She's not telling us everything."

Robynne didn't seem perturbed. "I wouldn't tell a complete stranger everything either." My hopes went up with that, but then she turned to me. "Still, we didn't come to you. You've come to us. So, if you want help, you need to tell us more."

Nosewise ambled over to swat my legs with his tail, encouraging me to reveal all.

I've been here a whole six hours, and I swear, they're really nice, his happy expression said.

I clenched and unclenched my hands, not convinced.

A man with dark hair and piercing black eyes jogged into camp at exactly that moment. *Really* piercing eyes that reminded me of an eagle focused on unsuspecting prey from a great distance.

"Alan," one of the men greeted him.

He strode breathlessly to Robynne, as if to report some critical news. But she stuck up a hand, keeping her focus on me.

"Why is this particular treasure so important?" she repeated.

Her tone went hard, and I didn't dare test her patience.

"Well, there's a lot of it, for starters," I said. "Enough to cover a good portion of the king's ransom."

Robynne waited, her eyes telegraphing, *What else?*

I reached into my pockets and pulled out the few pieces I'd taken with me. "This is just a fraction of what's in Nottingham now — all at the mercy of the sheriff."

I waited, sure the mention of the man would strike terror in their hearts. Everyone knew the sheriff of Nottingham was a ruthless tyrant loyal to Prince John…didn't they?

And yet a tiny smile played over Robynne's lips. What did she know that I didn't?

"*Acting* sheriff. No need to worry about him."

I pictured the kind gesture of the knight in the city. Huh. Were the rumors false, or was that a different man entirely?

"That's the thing," Alan cut in. "He's been called away."

Robynne's head whipped around so fast, I feared she would get a neck injury. "Say again?"

Alan nodded grimly. "The sheriff was called away this morning. By order of Prince John — some special assignment. Captain Giles is in command until Sir Guy of Gisborne arrives."

Gasps and concerned murmurs swept through the men, and Robynne's face fell. When she turned back to me, her upbeat mood was gone, replaced by tight lines of concern.

"Oh, and our guest here is wanted, too," Alan went on.

I frowned. "For what crime?"

"Any crime they make up," John grumbled. "Like with every man here."

"Well, that makes her one of us," one of the men joked.

I shot him a grateful smile.

John kicked the ground and muttered something. What was it with that man?

Robynne stirred the air with her hand. "What else makes the treasure special?"

The woman was like a bloodhound on a hot trail. And I was not in a position to delay any longer.

I drew the dagger I'd taken and held it high. "Some of the pieces in the collection are spelled."

John laughed. "Spelled? Like magic? You really believe that?"

I glared at him. Funny how quickly a habit could form.

To be honest, I'd been skeptical too. But my mistress had been adamant.

I turned the dagger this way and that, letting it reflect light with every sharp move. "Yes, magic. My mistress said this dagger is spelled to kill the king's worst enemies."

Robynne snorted. "Who might that be? There are so many..."

I shook my head. "Monsters. Unnatural creatures God didn't place on this earth."

"What, like ghosts?" John jeered.

When laughs ensued, I stamped the ground. God, I hated when men didn't take me seriously.

"No, I mean shifters. Werewolves. Werebears. All kinds of horrible creatures."

Everyone went dead quiet, staring. The light in the forest was patchy, but I swore several of the men paled. Robynne went still as a statue, and Alan's dark eyes went wide as an owl's.

Good. At least they took that seriously.

"This dagger is spelled to kill shifters," I explained. "Something nearly impossible to do."

When I cut the air with the dagger, several of the men jumped back, and even Robynne flinched.

"The king's enemies, you say?" Her voice was hard.

I nodded. "Like Sir Guy."

Gasps broke out, and I couldn't blame them.

"I was shocked when I learned that too," I admitted. "But it's true. Sir Guy is a wolf shifter. I saw him transform with my own eyes."

I half expected them to grill me on the details of how, what, where, and when, because how many people had seen shifters? Yet no one so much as peeped.

"What about Prince John?" Robynne asked, watching me closely.

"Well, he's the king's enemy, but I'm not sure if he's a shifter." Having made my point, I put the dagger away. "This isn't the only spelled piece. There are more."

"With what powers?" Robynne asked.

"I'm not sure," I said truthfully.

Well, almost truthfully. My mistress had slipped a ring off her own finger before I'd left home. *The Ring of Aquitaine,* she'd said, turning it reverently in her hands. *A ring that gives its bearer extraordinary powers.* Then she'd smiled mischievously. *But only if the bearer is a woman.*

I hadn't been able to find it in my rush to leave the carriage, but I wasn't overly concerned. The sheriff, Sir Guy, and every other powerful enemy of the king were men, so the ring posed little danger even if it fell into their hands.

I'd never considered its use in the hands of an ally, and I hadn't known Robynne Hood was a woman. If the ring really was magic, it might help her.

Then I gulped, wondering. Would it help me?

Robynne looked up, judging the fading light.

"All right. It's getting late, and we have much to discuss."

That *we* was aimed at her men, not me. But I wasn't exactly in a position to call the shots. All I could do was trust Robynne to do the right thing — such as launching a plan to steal the treasure from Nottingham.

Robynne pointed to John. "You. Take Willa to your place and set her up for the night, then bring her back for dinner."

Our protests drowned each other out.

"No!"

"Wait!"

Robynne stuck a finger at John. "You found her. You take care of her."

"But—" we both said at exactly the same time.

Robynne shook her head. "No buts."

"I don't need taking care of!" I insisted.

"I'm sure you don't, but this is our turf, and you do as we say." After that flat command, Robynne's voice grew softer. "I'm sure you're clever enough to understand why that's necessary."

I frowned. No, I wasn't here to double-cross Robynne and her men. But I supposed I wouldn't trust a complete stranger either. Still, being sent home with this man?

I implored Robynne with my eyes, but she just shooed us onward. "Come now. I'm sure you two can get along."

"I'm sure we can't," John muttered as he stomped off sullenly.

I followed, just as unhappy. Could I trust him? Could I trust anyone?

Nosewise, the traitor, stayed behind with Robert, leaving me to face my fate alone.

I pointed off the trail John led me along. "There. I can spend the night in that hollow."

He snorted. "Go on, then. Survive a night on your own."

"A night alone is better than a night with you."

"I couldn't agree more," he grumbled. "But Robynne is right. Much as I'd like to be rid of you forever, we need to keep an eye on you."

Somehow, the *rid of you forever* part cut straight to my heart.

I huffed. "Lest I steal some treasure, maybe? Or, wait. What if I refuse to steal some?"

He shot me a dirty look. "I didn't know you wanted it stolen."

And there we were, back where we'd started.

My emotions were in a similar state — torn between *I despise this man* and *I'd really like to get to know him better* — or simply to figure out *how* I knew him.

Still, it had been a hell of a day, and I had yet to face dinner with the Merry Men. So I followed John along a trail that headed upward, following the sweep of the land. Soon, we arrived at the base of a cliff, lit in golden hues by the first rays of sunset. When I touched the rock face, it exuded warmth absorbed throughout the day.

So, John Littlebrain had more sense than I'd thought. It was the perfect place to live, winter or summer, in fair or foul weather. A beautiful place, even, with a tidy path and a trickling stream. A naturally fortified, easily defensible place as well, I noted.

We passed a dark cave, then climbed ten steps to a shelter above. Some of the steps were natural, while others had been carved into the rock. And as for the shelter itself...

I looked around, impressed. John Little had done a hell of a job making a home for himself. The rock shelter was deep enough to offer protection from rain and wind, yet high enough to admit sunlight. An endless canopy of trees stretched away below, creating a carpet of green. One tree towered over the others, and I gaped, spotting a structure near the top.

"Whoa. Who lives up there?"

"Alan," John muttered, barely turning.

I marveled a moment longer, then took in my home for the night. The rock shelter was equipped in the simplest possible way — a fire pit, a bed on four low posts against one wall, some shelving against the other, and a tree stump for a seat. It occupied a prime position from which to appreciate the view, and I couldn't help picturing John sitting there, eyes closed, soaking in the last rays of the day.

Hell, I could picture *myself* sitting there soaking in the last rays of the day. Maybe even sharing that view.

I watched as John shook out a blanket, filled a jug with water, and arranged candles, setting me up for a comfortable night. Much more comfortable than necessary. The setting sun cast a warm glow over his face, and as I watched him move, something in me moved too.

The man was like a mountain lake, where quiet waters ran deep. Maybe there was more to the guy than I'd thought. Maybe he wasn't the fool I'd made him out to be. He couldn't have known about my plan for the treasure. In normal circumstances, I would have hailed him a hero for letting me keep it.

I went back to that moment in the carriage, when our eyes had locked, making my heart thump.

"What about you? Where will you sleep?" I asked, more softly than before.

He scowled and looked out over trees, shattering the magic spell. "As far from you as possible."

Chapter Six

JOHN

Waking early the next morning wasn't as hard as I expected. I'd spent the night in my cave in bear form, which normally helped me find deep sleep for hours. But my stupid beast spent the whole night pining for Willa and practically sprinted out to check on her at the crack of dawn.

I shifted to human form and dressed quickly. Not that Willa was waiting for me.

"Rise and shine?" she muttered, echoing my greeting.

The words had come out before I could stop them — all my bear's fault.

"I'm supposed to shine — now?" She stabbed a finger at the dim landscape. "How?"

Even after we finished breakfast with Robynne and the others, Willa and I had barely exchanged five words. As at dinner, Robynne invited Willa to sit with her — a huge relief to my human side. But to my bear...

Damn shame, the beast mourned. *I wanted her to sit with me.*

The stupid bear just wasn't getting the message. That was the problem with him. Very thick-headed and all too hopeful when it came to things like destiny. That woman was no more my destiny than Robert was my brother — thank goodness.

After breakfast, I pulled Robynne aside, trying to talk her into evicting Willa.

"Willa breaks all our rules. No outsiders. No women..."

Robynne nailed me with a sharp look. "Since when, no women?"

I hemmed and hawed. We'd had that rule before Robynne arrived and whipped our little band into shape.

"I think Willa breaks all *your* rules," Robynne said.

True, but rules had a purpose. Without them, society would break down. Even out in Sherwood Forest, rules were important. Especially the rules I made, dammit!

Still, I tried covering up. "I meant no humans."

"I see," Robynne said dryly. "Normally, I would agree, but the circumstances are exceptional."

Yes, they were. Willa was not just a human, an outsider, and a woman. She also hated me with a passion.

Exceptional circumstances, for sure.

"I hate humans," I finally admitted.

Robynne snorted. "You lived your whole life in a remote cottage, and the one time you ventured near a town, you ended up in a trap. How does that make all humans bad?"

That, and a few other negative experiences I wasn't about to share — especially the one that had branded me an outlaw.

I rammed my hands into my pockets. "They just are."

Robynne gave me a look.

"I don't trust her," I finally said.

Robynne chuckled. "Neither do I... yet. But I like her."

I snorted. What was there to like?

To love... my inner bear whispered dreamily.

Robynne turned and whistled for everyone's attention. All the camp dogs — plus Nosewise — ran up, wagging their tails. She laughed, petting them, then straightened. "All right, everybody. Listen up. I have a plan."

"I had a plan too," Willa muttered.

I turned my eyes to heaven. Boy, did she have a chip on her shoulder.

Quickly, efficiently, Robynne laid it all out. We would send a party to Nottingham to locate the loot. If there was any way to steal it immediately, we would. In any case, we had to get moving. If Alan had heard correctly, Sir Guy of Gisborne was already on his way to snatch the treasure.

"We can't let him get it," Willa insisted. "Not him, and not Prince John."

She hated both with a passion — one of the rare things we had in common.

We have lots in common, my bear insisted. *We both like being outdoors. We can both fight with a staff. . .*

I rolled my eyes. *We both have two eyes, ten fingers, and one nose. . .*

"We'll do our best to prevent it falling into the hands of Sir Guy," Robynne said grimly, then proceeded with the details.

"What?" I gawked a moment later.

"What?" Willa protested at the same time.

"You're part of the reconnaissance party," Robynne pointed to me. She shook her head at Willa. "You're not."

We both protested, but Robynne was adamant. As she spoke, I dug a long furrow in the ground with the heel of my boot. I hated town. I hated people. I distrusted women.

So, it was good news that Willa wasn't assigned to the party going into town. Right?

Everything had been fine until she'd come along. She accused me of ruining her plan? Well, she ruined my quiet, comfortable routine.

And yet, the longer I spent around her, the more I yearned for her.

"But. . . but. . ." Willa tried.

Robynne shook her head so firmly, even Willa quit.

"There's no time to waste. You, you, and you." Robynne pointed to Alan, Martin, and me. "We're leaving in five minutes."

∞∞∞∞

I strode out of camp as resolutely as Robynne. I had to, because something kept pulling me back, and it was all I could do to keep moving.

Can't leave her! my bear protested.

The truth was, it hurt to leave Willa, the same way it hurt to see her glum and frustrated.

But, hell. That was one truth I was not ready to examine. So I turned my back and followed Robynne to Nottingham. We covered the distance in less than the usual two hours, split up to covertly enter the city through different gates, then took up positions around the market square.

The place was bustling, not so much due to the market as the weather. Dark clouds swirled on the horizon — a sure storm, and a severe one. Everyone hurried to get the pick of the goods and bring them home before the deluge hit.

Robynne, in a plain peasant's dress and cloak, fit right in. Alan and Martin did too. My bulky frame made it harder to blend in, so my job was to hang back, keep an overview, and support the others if things went wrong. I also kept my ears perked for the latest news. Not a hard ask since the town was buzzing with it.

"I heard Sir Guy has a hundred men marching on Nottingham now," a passing woman said.

A hundred? God, I hoped not.

"A pity the sheriff is away. He would stand up to Sir Guy, but I doubt Captain Giles will," the man beside her grumbled.

"I just hope Sir Guy will move on quickly and leave us be," someone else fretted.

The woman snorted. "Sure — he'll stay just long enough to get his hands on the treasure that came in yesterday."

Her friend glanced toward the castle, where I assumed the carriage had been brought. "You'd think it foolhardy to send so many valuables in one batch, but somehow, they made it through Sherwood Forest without being robbed."

I dug my boot heel into the ground. Yeah. *Somehow*, like me letting it go.

A moment later, Alan's voice sounded in my head. *Rumor has it the sheriff locked the loot in the keep before he was called away.*

Robynne's furrowed brow revealed her concern, but she managed to stick to business.

Surely he wouldn't be that obvious.

He wouldn't have had much time to find an alternative, Alan pointed out.

We all waited for Robynne's thoughts. Every man in our band knew she had a secret informant close to the sheriff. I was the only one who knew that informant was the sheriff himself. Either way, Robynne always came through with insider knowledge at exactly the right time.

Which made the ensuing silence all the more deafening.

Where? Martin prompted her.

Frustration and concern registered in Robynne's reply. *I don't know.*

Now that was a first.

We waited silently for Robynne to formulate Plan B — or C or D, because Robynne always thought several steps ahead. Still, this time, she seemed stumped.

All right, she finally said. *Alan, find a place to shift to eagle form and fly over the keep. See what you can discover and report back. Martin, you snoop around the parade grounds. John and I will stay here and learn what we can.*

Alan and Martin set off from opposite sides of the market square. I wandered around the perimeter, thinking, listening. Where would I hide the loot if I were in a hurry?

A well, my bear tried. *A prison cell. Under the secret honey stash in the castle kitchen...*

A trumpet blared out, and every head in the square turned.

"He's coming!" someone shouted. "He's coming!"

I hoped that meant the sheriff, but the hairs standing on the back of my neck said otherwise.

"Sir Guy of Gisborne! Clear the way for Sir Guy!" one of the guards boomed.

Everyone rushed for cover, knocking over sacks of potatoes and sending chickens aflutter. Horseshoes clanged over cobblestones, and a moment later, thirty mounted men thundered into the square. The townsfolk pressed back, barely avoiding being trampled.

Trumpets blared in greeting, helping Sir Guy make a grand entrance. He galloped in on a coal-black stallion that pranced in place, then reared dramatically.

Of course, Sir Guy could have ridden in on a lame pony and still made a splash. I'd never seen eyes as dark or as piercing.

Nor had I ever sensed so much evil packed into one person. His nostrils twitched, giving a hint of the wolf shifter within. A sword glinted at his side, boasting of all the blood it had drawn. How much of that had been deserved, and how much innocent?

All in all, Sir Guy was about as bad as bad came. But a carriage clattered in next, and when the woman within peered out...

"Lady Thornton," someone gasped.

I leaned back, swallowing a curse.

"Who?" someone whispered.

The answer came in a low, fearful hush. "Sir Guy's sister. A widow."

Dark, calculating eyes darted this way and that, and her features grew even more pinched.

Widow? Rumor said she'd bumped off her first — and her second — husband. I'd always dismissed the stories that Lady Thornton was twice as dangerous as her brother, but one look made me a believer.

I drew back, glad for the pungent tanner's pit nearby. Shifters could sense — and smell — other shifters. If either of them spotted me now...

Robynne stood across from me in the square, watching Sir Guy and Lady Thornton.

Shit. Her curse sounded in my mind.

Yes, that pretty much summed things up.

Sir Guy dismounted and paced toward Captain Giles, pinning him with those eerie, obsidian eyes. Huge spurs punctuated every step with a metallic ring. *Stomp, stomp, clink. Stomp, stomp, clink...*

Robynne stepped backward, calling into our minds. *We need to get out of here before we're spotted. Use any gate but the north. Go, everyone. Go!*

With that, she slipped into the crowd, impossible, as always, to spot.

I waited, letting her get a head start. All around me, townsfolk chattered, jostling me again and again. When yet another bumped me from behind, I half turned, stifling a growl.

Then a honeysuckle-and-rose scent hit my nose, and I froze, watching a boy wade through the crowd. The boy who'd bumped me. Or was it...?

Willa! my bear cheered.

Chapter Seven

JOHN

I frowned. Wait. What was Willa doing in Nottingham?

It's a good thing to be close to our mate, my bear protested.

I started after Willa, but the moment that thought registered, I stumbled.

Our what?

Our mate, my bear said. *It's destiny.*

My chest squeezed — from joy? Despair? Disbelief?

Joy, my bear beamed.

I shook my head. No, despair. I'd never believed in destined mates—

Well, believe now, my bear cut in.

—and even if I did, there was no way my mate could be a human as stubborn as Willa.

Robynne's faint voice cut into my mind. *Get moving, John. Use the west gate. Sir Guy's rear guard are heading for the east gate.*

I blinked, torn. The west gate wasn't far. But Willa was headed east. Why hadn't she heeded Robynne's orders and waited in the forest, dammit?

Because she's not one to wait around, my bear hummed proudly. *She takes matters into her own hands.*

Exactly the problem. I didn't want or need a headstrong, overbearing human in my life. Especially one aiming for disaster at the east gate.

Stop her! my bear growled. *Save her!*

Something told me Willa would be about as cooperative in being saved as she'd been about being robbed. But an irresistible force drove me onward. My bear pointed the way through the dense crowd, navigating by feel, not sight or scent. I shivered, because tracking that way shouldn't be possible — unless I was tracking my mate.

What's taking so long? Get out! Robynne urged.

I gulped, following Willa. *New plan. I have to stick with Willa.*

Have to fit, because my limbs were acting on their own, not heeding my orders.

Robynne cursed. *I told her to wait in camp.*

As if we needed further proof how impossible Willa was.

The crowd thinned out ahead, and I finally spotted her racing toward. . . the latrine near a corner of the city walls?

Forget it, Robynne ordered. *Get out while you still can. Sir Guy's men are locking down the city, one street at a time.*

Won't leave my mate, my bear cried.

But I couldn't blurt that to the others, so I cast around for some other excuse.

Willa has the spelled dagger, I finally said. *We can't let it fall into enemy hands.*

Robynne cursed again. *You're right. Get her and the dagger out of there. But stay away from the east gate. Sir Guy's men are there now.*

Exactly where Willa was headed. I sighed. If she really was my mate, destiny hated me.

Willa turned a corner and disappeared. I raced after her, just in time to see her duck into a shed. I followed, throwing the door open. A heartbeat later, a sharp blade swung at my stomach.

"Hey!" I jumped back.

The spelled dagger missed, but Willa's glare hit me like a physical thing.

I took another step away from the blade. "Watch it!"

She scowled. "What are you doing, sneaking up on me? Go away! You'll ruin everything — again."

Of course, she had to rub that in.

"Sir Guy is here. We have to get away while we can."

Clear instructions even a child could understand. Yet what did Willa do?

Agile as a monkey, she climbed into the rafters and grappled with something.

"I need that ring..."

"What ring? We need to get out of here. Sir Guy's troops are pouring into town."

"From the north gate," Willa muttered, as if that was much comfort.

"East gate too," I corrected.

She glanced down sharply. "How do you know?"

Ha. Even if I wanted to explain, I couldn't just say, *I'm a shifter. All of us in Sherwood Forest are. We can communicate in ways humans can't. Oh, and watch out with that spelled dagger, please.*

"Long story. We have to get out before it's too late."

"I need that ring."

She rummaged through a bundle of small treasures. Gold glinted, and silver clinked as necklaces tangled. Part of the treasure?

I gawked. "Where did you get that?"

"Long story," she muttered.

I cursed, peeking out the door. The coast was clear so far, but I could hear the stomp of soldiers in the distance.

"Dammit, it's not here." Willa thrust the bundle back into the rafters and jumped down. The minute she landed, I tugged her out the door.

"Let's go."

She yanked her arm free. "Don't touch me. And don't tell me what to do."

She was tiny. I was big. It would be so, so easy to throw her over my shoulder and just go. And it was so, so hard to patch my frayed patience and reason with her.

"Fine. Decide for yourself. But given that the west gate is our closest option..."

A blast of cold wind blew down the street, reminding us a storm was approaching. I took off, praying she would follow.

Or maybe praying she wouldn't. Willa muddled my mind so badly, I couldn't decide.

She hesitated, but a moment later, footsteps sounded. She was following me.

Not for long. My bear grinned as Willa passed and took the lead.

I rolled my eyes. Of course. Why would a woman follow a man when she could charge headlong into danger?

Without warning, she halted, and I plowed into her from behind.

"Watch out!" I grabbed her shoulders.

Little zings of energy ran through my veins, making my body warm and hazy. My mind, too.

Told you she's our mate, my bear cooed.

"*You* watch out," Willa hissed. "They're coming. We have to backtrack." She snapped her fingers in front of my face. "Hello? Hello? Focus, already!"

I wished I could, but I could barely think, move, or breathe. Not with warm, fuzzy sensations invading every corner of my body.

"Hurry up," she muttered, shoving me.

I stumbled, then fell into step behind her.

We charged back into the market square. Sir Guy, Lady Thornton, and dozens of troops took up most of the space, but it was easy to lose ourselves among the gaping city folk.

"This way." Willa tugged me along as if heading to the west gate had been *her* idea.

We pushed through the crowd, up a street, and onto the main artery that connected the east and west gates. There, we slowed. Running would call attention to us. Walking, we might get away with.

I didn't dare look back at Sir Guy's rear guard. I didn't have to, thanks to the din they made. They'd swept through the east gate and branched out like a flood, covering the northeast corner of Nottingham. Ahead of us stood the open west gate, our only hope. But the local guards marched forward to greet Sir Guy's forces, trapping us between them.

"Dammit..." Willa looked for a shop or alley to duck into.

I did too, but there was nothing. Just a row of half-timbered houses crowding both sides of the road.

The guards at the gate approached, and I was sure they would drag us in for questioning — or worse. Meanwhile, the martial sound of marching grew louder behind us. There was no way out. Absolutely no way. Except...

A crazy idea hit me. A truly insane one. But my bear side loved it, and before I had time to think...

I pressed Willa against the nearest wall and leaned in as if to kiss her.

And, oops. I didn't just lean. I really did kiss her.

Soldiers snickered and marched by without bothering us, except for wolf whistles and stupid comments like, *You show her, boy* and *So hungry, and it's not even lunch.*

But all that was a hundred miles away, because the kiss transported me to a floating cloud of bliss. One where my arms were wrapped around Willa and hers around me while our lips gently danced. Every movement was soft and dreamlike, and my feet felt like they'd left the ground.

It wasn't a kiss so much as a door to another world, all beautiful and perfect.

Willa's hands cupped my face, angling it for a better fit.

"You there!" someone yelled.

We broke apart, seizing the breath we'd skipped.

It was one of the soldiers calling to a comrade, not us.

I blinked at Willa, still teetering on the threshold of that dreamworld. I kissed her again, bringing us more *in* than *out.* But when the last of the guards passed behind us, Willa nudged me back.

I blinked, half expecting an angry slap. But Willa looked just as off-kilter as I felt.

"They left the gate unguarded," she whispered. "Now's our chance."

It was, and I knew it. Still, part of me burned to fall back into that kiss, consequences be damned.

In the end, raindrops propelled us into action. That brewing storm was finally breaking.

Behind us, hunched guards conferred with Sir Guy's troops. Ahead, the gate stood open.

We jog-walked the first few steps, then sprinted as the rain increased. We hesitated in the shelter of the arched gateway, then darted out.

"Hurry," Willa whispered.

We ran over the wooden bridge spanning the moat, then down the muddy road. Within ten steps, we were soaked from both directions — freezing rain from above, frigid splashes underfoot.

"We need to get out of sight. Head for the forest," Willa called over the sound of splattering rain.

Water dripped down my nose as I pointed through the deluge. "Too late."

Sir Guy's troops had fanned out, cutting off all paths between Nottingham and the forest.

Where are you, John? Robynne called into my mind.

Our mental connection gave me a glimpse of her surroundings — the edge of the forest, thank goodness. She, Alan, and Martin had made it.

Outside the west gate, I replied. *We'll circle around as soon as we can. But right now...*

Willa touched my hand, and despite the cold, the rain, and imminent danger all around, I felt hope and warmth.

Hope and warmth that terrified me because of what they suggested.

Mate, my bear hummed.

I took a deep breath. One thing at a time. We needed shelter — the sooner, the better.

As usual, Willa was ahead of me. She took off at a jog, heading west. "Any idea where we can go?"

I jogged beside her, considering the options. None were good. Not when it came to providing shelter a safe distance from our enemies.

Deciding the second option was the priority, I picked up the pace. "One idea. Whether it's a good one..." I didn't dare meet Willa's eyes. "Time will tell."

Chapter Eight

WILLA

I cursed Sir Guy while sloshing through the rain and mud. I cursed myself. I cursed John for being right about my plan being too hasty. But desperate times called for desperate measures, so what choice had I had?

Okay, maybe I shouldn't have followed John — er, Robynne — into Nottingham. But I couldn't have known Sir Guy would show up at the worst possible time.

We'd escaped, but I'd had to abandon my search for the treasure. Worse, I'd had to suffer through John's out-of-nowhere kiss — a horrible, demeaning, and unnecessary measure that would haunt me for the rest of my days...

...or spice up my dreams for the rest of my nights. Because, wow. How often did a girl get a kiss like that? One that started fast, then slowed down, since a kiss like that was too good to rush. One that made my eyes go wide, then slowly slide to half-mast, because it was that good. From starting a little cold, it had heated way, way up, making my hands sneak around John's waist and my lips part.

That kiss affected John as much as me, because his expression went just as blank as mine, then turned to *Wait! Please don't stop* when we finally eased apart.

So, wow. A kiss like none I'd ever enjoyed before. Would I ever enjoy one that good again?

My heart panged.

Then my foot landed in a puddle, and the cold splash yanked me back to my senses. No, no, no. There was nothing desirable about that kiss. It was horrible, demeaning, and unnecessary, and I had to remember that.

I glanced at the big, muscled, warrior-type striding beside me. Yes, I really, *really* had to remember that.

"How far is that abbey?" I asked over the rain.

His expression was grim. "Five miles."

I looked around. We needed shelter much sooner. Sir Guy's men were already combing the surroundings, and we'd had to zig and zig half a dozen times since we'd left Nottingham to avoid bumping into them. Visibility was poor, and those men were just as miserable as we were, but we still couldn't afford to hang around.

A harness jingled, and we both whirled. The rider was looking left, so we darted right, into a small stand of trees. I crouched, shivering, waiting for him to pass.

"Over here," John whispered.

The tree he indicated was so big, it would have taken ten men to circle. Once upon a time, lightning must have struck the upper half of the tree, which now lay folded at a sharp angle to the trunk.

"There's shelter if we back in far enough," John whispered, indicating the hollow trunk.

There was, as it turned out, but only for one. John pressed into the space, but that left me out in the freezing rain.

"Fine," I muttered, looking around for a different nook. I tried several, but rain poured into every one.

"It's dry in here," John hissed once the soldier had passed. "Get in."

I shook my head. *Get in* meant *squeeze in* — right into his embrace.

Forget it, I tried muttering, though my teeth were chattering too much to make the word clear.

"Willa," he called.

Something in his soft, wistful tone melted me, and I gave in, backing stiffly into his arms... his chest... pretty much his lap. Which was a lot like that kiss.

Electrifying.

Er, horrible, demeaning, and...something else I couldn't remember in my cold, wet state. We were squeezed into a tiny space, our bodies mashed together everywhere they oughtn't be, having effects they really oughtn't.

But, hell. I had to stay dry, right?

Happy little sparks traveled to every part of my body. A cheery hum set into my ears, as if Cupid were singing a love song to us both. I sighed, closed my eyes, and relaxed for the first time that day.

A moment later, my eyes flew open. Wait. I was neither relaxed, nor comfortable. Was I?

"I thought you said it was dry," I muttered at the droplets hitting my elbow.

"Semidry," John admitted.

We both peered silently out into the rain.

Semi and *dry* were both exaggerations, I decided, but less wet than the downpour an inch to either side.

It occurred to me that if I only had an inch to either side, and John was that much bigger than me...

I twisted to look up. "Wait. Are you staying dry at all?"

Judging by the rivulets running off his shoulders, no. His voice was probably the only thing about him that was dry.

"Semi," was all he said.

I hunched down in the shelter he created for me. How could a man be such an oaf, yet still be so considerate? Was it the kiss that had somehow shifted things between us, or maybe our common enemy? Because now, we felt more like accomplices than adversaries.

"Maybe I can find my own shelter," I offered, though I knew my prospects were slim.

"Or you could stay put and keep quiet," came his droll reply.

Another wordless minute passed with no letup in the deluge.

"Thank you," I whispered, half hoping he wouldn't hear.

He sighed. "You're welcome. Besides, I owe you."

"For what?"

"For getting me out of that river."

I frowned. He was keeping score?

"You're not supposed to help so that people owe you," I said. "You're supposed to help because it's the right thing to do."

"And the right thing to do is pay back what I owe."

"When it comes to money, yes. But how do you weigh up other things?" Twisting to face him brought me partly into the rain, but I didn't care. "Does keeping me dry equate to saving your life?"

"Fine, fine. I still owe you," he grumbled.

"That's not my point."

"Oh, for God's sake." He threw up his hands. "Fine. I do not owe you. I'll just keep you dry because it's the right thing to do." He opened his arms, motioning me sternly closer.

I held my ground for about ten seconds. Then, with a look that said *Only because I have no choice*, I snuggled — er, forced myself — back into his dry embrace.

"Semidry," I muttered a minute later.

I couldn't see him roll his eyes from my position, but I was sure he did.

"Just be glad you're so small," he growled.

I stuck an elbow into his ribs. "I'm not small."

"Why are you so touchy?"

Ha. This guy was accusing *me* of being touchy?

"I'm not touchy. It's just a fact. It's best not to rely on men."

"And yet, you're dry."

I shrugged. "Semi. So far."

The rain continued to fall in sheets, with chilly little rivers springing up on the slope on either side of our tree. It was only a question of time before they seeped into our hiding place.

"Maybe it's women you can't rely on," John murmured.

His low, growly voice was alluringly close to my ear. Which meant his lips couldn't be far either.

My heart skipped a beat.

Still, I kept up an uncompromising front. "Women don't start wars. Women don't rape, pillage, or steal — or at least, very, very rarely. When they do steal, it's not for personal gain so much as the need to feed hungry children."

A long, quiet pause ensued until he murmured, "Okay, you have a point there."

I quietly savored that small triumph.

"But you have to agree, the exceptions are pretty awful. Like Lady Thornton." His tone hinted at some bitter personal betrayal — and not by Lady Thornton.

"True," I granted. "But she's an outlier. Take Robynne as an example. She's a woman. Is she not to be trusted?"

"Robynne is an exception."

Funny how that cut me. As if I wanted the honor of being an exception too. I wanted that respect, that trust.

"Exceptional how?" I demanded.

John thought for a moment, then shrugged. "She's honest. Smart, too — smarter than any of us — and loyal as hell."

Despite his gruff tone, his words made me soften a bit. Obviously, John was loyal too — and one of those rare men who could treat a woman as his equal or even his superior.

I sighed a little inside. If only I had someone that loyal to me.

"You mean, she's loyal to King Richard?"

He nodded. "And to us. Her men, I mean."

Her men. Plural. Loyal. A team.

Lucky woman, part of me sighed.

But then I caught myself. It was better — safer, easier — to be my own one-woman team. That way, the only person who could let me down was me.

Somehow, the thought wasn't all that inspiring.

Another long silence stretched in relative peace. Obviously, we were better off when neither of us spoke.

Which shouldn't have struck me as such a sad thought, but it did.

So I was inexplicably glad when John eventually said, "Back in town, that...that..."

That kiss? I nearly filled in.

Amazing. Delicious. Stunning, the back of my mind hummed.

John finished his sentence, deflating my ego. "...that man..."

So much for amazing, delicious, and stunning. Had the kiss been just business to him?

"Sir Guy, I mean," John said. "In camp, you said he was a shifter. How do you know?"

Ugly memories popped into my mind, and I struggled to keep my voice even.

"Ever since King Richard left for the Crusades, Prince John has raised taxes, and his collectors add their own fee on top of that. A year ago, my mother threatened to complain to authorities like Sir Guy."

John waited for me to go on.

I scowled as I finished. "The tax collectors just laughed and said, *What do you think Sir Guy is?*" I shook my head, as angry now as I'd been then. "Not *who* but *what*. Then they transformed into wolves right in front of us and advanced, step by step, snarling and slobbering."

I formed fists with my hands, trying not to show how terrified I'd been that day. The shifters had targeted my mother and younger sister first, then focused on my elder sister and me when we'd jumped in to intervene. If it hadn't been for another tax collector arriving to hurry the shifters along — not because murdering innocent souls was wrong, but because they were running late — I was sure we would have died a horrible death.

I skipped to the end. "When they left to report to Sir Guy, I saw him shift too."

Nothing intimidated my mother, but those shifters had, and I would never forget how she'd locked every door and shutter in the house, gathered us up in her arms, and shaken in fear.

The *wild animal* aspect was only part of what frightened us. Their sadistic, power-hungry side was even worse, perhaps because it was purely human.

"Werewolves. Monsters." I touched my dagger. "I'm not sure I believe this weapon is spelled, but who knows? It might come in handy."

Truthfully, that was a lot of bravado, because I never, ever wanted to take on a wolf shifter with nothing more than a dagger. Heck, I never, ever wanted to take on a wolf shifter at all.

My gesture made the scabbard move, and when it bumped John, he flinched. *Really* flinched, like he was truly afraid.

I hid a chuckle. It had probably come a little too close to his groin. Lord knew how protective men got around *that.*

The thing was, the dagger had heated up when Sir Guy had arrived in Nottingham. I'd brushed my hand against it unconsciously, then nearly jumped at the warmth emanating from the blade. Which made me inclined to believe in magic. And if the dagger really was spelled, then what about that ring?

The Ring of Aquitaine, my mistress had said, turning it reverently in her hands. *A ring that gives its bearer extraordinary powers. But only if the bearer is a woman.*

"Lady Thornton," I cursed.

"She's even worse than her brother," John muttered.

My mind went into overdrive. As a woman, Lady Thornton could tap into the ring's extraordinary power and use it for ill gain.

I glanced toward Nottingham, even though the trees and mist hid my view. The ring was still there, mixed in among other treasures. What if Sir Guy and Lady Thornton were sorting through them now?

"I bet she's a shifter, too," I whispered. "A monster, like Sir Guy. Evil. Cruel. Ruthless."

"Humans can be cruel too," John pointed out.

"True. I've heard the sheriff is as bad as any shifter."

"That was the old sheriff. There's a new one now. Well, acting sheriff. He's proven to be very fair."

I shrugged. "Power corrupts, you know. And imagine how bad that is when it's a shifter."

John didn't say a word, and once again, the silence stretched.

It couldn't be far past midday, but the light was gloomy and the rain so intense, I could barely see beyond the trees.

The damp cold crept steadily into my bones, making me shiver harder.

"Stay close," John ordered, tugging me back.

I wanted to protest — truly, I did — but his warmth beckoned like a fireplace, and I found myself snuggling in. That put John's arms loosely around my waist, though he had the decency to rest his hands on his own thighs.

The thighs nestled around my body right then. I gulped, fighting off inappropriate thoughts.

"Well, this rain can't last all day," I tried.

John sighed. "This is Nottinghamshire. It can and probably will."

I stared glumly out into the downpour. "At least it keeps Sir Guy's men from searching too thoroughly. But we ought to keep a lookout, I suppose."

"I am keeping a lookout," he growled, all touchy again.

"There are two of us. We can take turns. You know, cooperate." I forced the word out.

"I'll keep watch," he muttered in that *My suffering knows no limits* tone.

I held out a hand. "As if anyone is fool enough to be out in this."

"We still need to keep watch," he replied. "It's not safe here among these humans — er, hamlets."

"That's why we need to take turns. At some point, you'll get tired. Maybe even sleepy."

The man was a fierce, powerful giant, yet my imagination served up an image of him slumbering as peacefully as a baby. So sweet, so vulnerable, that I felt the urge to protect him.

He laughed. "We take turns keeping watch in camp, and I know every trick when it comes to staying awake."

This, I had to hear. "Such as?"

He dipped close and whispered right in my ear. "Think of all the sex you've ever had. In detail."

And, whoosh — the glowing embers of desire stoked by our proximity blazed into an all-out inferno.

"I doubt my list is as long as yours," I replied, sounding more prim than I had any right to.

His sinful laugh went right to my core. "Maybe. Maybe not."

Now I regretted asking, because I hated the thought of him with another woman. How long was his list, anyway? Longer than mine, I was certain.

In the silence that followed, the sound of rain took on a downright steamy undertone. A good thing we weren't in a cozy, atmospheric room with a fireplace and a big, warm bed. I might forget that I had to stay on guard around him.

Then again, the cold, slurpy mud around my feet made me rethink that.

Still, the *think of sex* trick worked, as I concluded hours later. The rain continued to fall in monotonous sheets, and John really did nod off for a while. I could tell by the way his chin lolled on my head. A feeling I liked much too much, and one that intruded into the memories I'd summoned for my watch — memories of my hot night with sweet, well-built Nelson, the blacksmith's son. So much that visions of Nelson moving over, under, and in me blurred with visions of John.

I cleared my throat and sat straighter every time I caught myself at it, but John kept sneaking into my dreams. Damn that man! Damn my libido!

When John woke sometime later, the afternoon was still dreary, and the rain still drummed the earth continuously.

The rumbly sound John made upon waking up was like a bear shaking himself out of hibernation. He didn't say a word at first, and neither did I, but a prickly feeling at the edge of my mind made me wonder if he was trying to read my thoughts.

Ha. As if I would ever let him in there.

Then he frowned — I couldn't see it, but I swore I could feel it — and grumbled, "Nelson?"

I froze. Whoa. Wait a minute.

Then, whew. I realized it wasn't mind reading. I must have whispered the name aloud.

I let out a dreamy sigh, just to annoy him. "Nelson..."

He snorted, and I bet if Nelson were there, they would have beaten their chests or boasted about the size of their man parts.

I rolled my eyes. Men!

I stuck a hand out into the freezing rain, as much to cool my libido as to test the conditions.

"Maybe we should get going," I suggested.

Sir Guy's men had probably given up their search by then, but they would be out again once the rain petered out.

"Maybe we should," the hulk behind me murmured.

It was a lot like talking to a boulder, or at least the way I imagined a boulder would sound, all low and gritty.

I shook out one leg, then the other, and cautiously stepped out of our hideaway. John followed, pointing west.

"That way."

A few steps later, I caught him side-eyeing me.

"What?"

He frowned, though it was a while before he spoke. "Seriously? Nelson?"

I laughed, delighted to have annoyed him. I answered in my lowest, sultriest voice.

"Seriously, baby. Nelson."

His brow furrowed even more deeply, and he stomped ahead with a manly swagger that said, *I could outdo Nelson.*

I couldn't resist studying his ass for the next few steps, and I might have licked my lips once or twice. Because, yes — I bet he could.

Not that I was interested in confirming that, I reminded myself. Not in the slightest.

Chapter Nine

JOHN

Nelson? my bear grumbled.

Whoever he was, I hated the guy.

I hated him all the way to Winslow Abbey, five bone-soaking miles later.

The storm gradually abated, though the thought only made me laugh bitterly.

A storm? That was Willa. A woman that fiery had all the makings of a perfect storm of *drama* and *complicated*. She and that shithead Nelson.

The bad news was I'd read it in her mind, which shouldn't have been possible — unless we were destined for each other.

The good news was, we were heading to a monastery. Maybe that would help cool off my unwelcome ardor. After all, the place was supposed to be sin-free.

A moment later, I sighed. *Supposed* to be.

Willa looked over at me. "What?"

I shook my head. "Nothing."

She didn't utter a word, but her eye roll said it all. *Men!*

As we walked, the rain eased, and the sound was gradually replaced by chirps of the few birds brave enough to venture from their nests. My clothes and hair were plastered to my skin, keeping me in a perpetual chill. If only I could shift to bear form and enjoy the instant warmth of my fur! But with Willa around, I couldn't.

Shifters are monsters. Inhuman. Her words echoed in my mind.

I shouldn't care what an ignorant human thought, but still. Those words cut deep.

I flexed my hand — the injured one — and thought back to that day that had put me forever in Willa's debt. A debt I'd tried to pay back, only to incur her ire and a new debt when she'd hauled me out of the brook. So, I'd done my best to keep her dry in the rain—

Semidry, my bear butted in.

Okay, to keep her semidry in the rain, but that didn't really pay much back.

We helped her escape Nottingham, my bear pointed out.

Yes, with that out-of-nowhere kiss. The one that still sent flames licking through my veins.

My lips twitched, and I yearned to do it again. I yearned to touch her again, even somewhere safe, like her perfect hips.

My gaze wandered there, only for me to pale again. Maybe not such a safe place, because that was where she strapped her dagger. But, heck. Willa was probably deadly with a normal blade. What did it matter if this one was spelled?

It mattered, because she didn't know about my bear side. And she couldn't find out, because that would make her despise me.

I suppressed a heavy sigh.

When we crested a rise, Willa motioned to the monastery complex ahead.

"So, an abbey? What makes this a safe place?"

I paused, taking it in. Stout walls formed a huge square with the church as its centerpiece and other, more modest structures around the edges: the cloisters, the monks' quarters, the abbot's house, and so on.

I made my way down toward a small chapel, one of the few buildings outside the abbey walls.

"We have a contact here."

Willa looked skeptical, but she bounded along beside me through the tall, wet grass.

"Good thing we're already drenched," she quipped.

I hid a smile. She had a way of looking on the bright side of things — except when it came to me, maybe. But I was starting to worry, because she'd been in those cold, wet clothes all day. As a shifter, I wouldn't fall sick, but Willa could.

The grassy slope bottomed out in a field surrounding the abbey — covered in wheat in summer, now as dreary as the weather. Open terrain, in other words. We approached stealthily — and boy, was Willa good at that. She was so quiet, I kept turning to check where she was, only to find her half a step away.

Eventually, we arrived at the chapel, and I pulled the door open. It creaked so loudly, I winced. We slipped inside, where vaulted ceilings and dozens of flickering candles created an entirely different atmosphere from the cold, gray nothingness we'd ghosted through all day.

"Wow," Willa murmured. "I've never been particularly religious, but just the promise of being warm and dry could make me a convert." Then she thought for a moment. "Huh. I bet that's half the attraction for some folks." Then she peeked toward the door and leaned in, keeping her voice low. "So, your contact...?"

"One of the monks here. Hopefully, he spotted us coming."

I sat in one of the pews, letting my focus drift off in the heart of a candle.

Much as she had back at the tree, Willa hesitated, then slid in beside me.

"We snuck in. How would he spot us?" she whispered.

I burned to tell her the truth. *He's a shifter, like me, with ultrakeen senses. Oh, and by the way, we shifters aren't all as bad as you think. You can trust us.*

You can trust me, my bear added mournfully.

"He comes through here several times a day," I explained. "It's his job to keep the candles burning."

She snorted. "Hell of a job."

I shushed her, pointing to the cross at the altar. "Watch your language."

For exactly three seconds, weighty silence reigned. Then we both broke into laughter.

"Shh! Shh!" Willa tried, though she was just as loud as I was.

It was silly, but a good laugh was just what I needed after a miserable day.

What we both needed, my bear grinned, watching Willa contort.

Her eyes shone, anchoring a huge smile and a hooting laugh most women would stifle. But not Willa.

Laughter, like warm soup, fluffy puppies, and crackling campfires, had a way of breaking tension, and the next minutes passed in amiable silence. Willa even slid close enough to warm my side. Okay, to warm her own side, more likely, but my bear rumbled happily.

She trusts me. She likes me.

Much as I reminded myself she was just cold and desperate, the thought grew on me.

I like her too, my bear continued.

The door behind us creaked open, and we jumped apart like forbidden lovers.

"Tuck." I greeted the young friar with a nod.

"Hello, John. And hello, miss."

"Willa." She introduced herself before I could.

Tuck flashed that perfect grin of his — the one that made women swoon and consider joining a nearby convent — making me hate the handsome lion shifter for the first time. He had it all. Good looks… athlete's build… two functioning hands, and ten nimble fingers…

Then I considered the flip side. Tuck was also training for a job that would bind him to celibacy for eternity. No, thank you. Not with a woman like Willa to—

I cut the thought off there.

"You've come to pray, no doubt." Tuck faked a look of piety.

"Um, yes," I replied. "We pray for a place to take shelter for a day or two. Somewhere Sir Guy — er, the devil — won't find us."

His eyes lit up at the hint of trouble. "So, you're the ones they're after. Four soldiers came asking about you earlier today."

I tensed, but Tuck flapped a hand, unconcerned. "They're in the dining hall, not budging from the fire — or their pitcher of ale." Then he went serious. "Still, we have to be careful. Follow me."

I whispered a warning before he reached the door. "Listen, Tuck. This could be dangerous for you."

His eyes danced. "You promise?"

Willa chuckled.

"I mean it," I insisted. Tuck was a good man and crucial to Robynne's scheme. Taking from the rich and giving to the poor wasn't as simple as it sounded, and Tuck was a key link in our delivery chain.

"I mean it, too," he assured me. "Eat, pray, sleep, repeat is killing me. Day after day, week after week, month after month, year after year..." He trailed off on a mournful note, then forced a weak grin. "Okay, it's only been four months, eighteen days, and six hours. Not that I'm counting..."

After peeking in both directions, he led us outside, then pointed the way before heading in a different direction. Following his instructions, Willa and I snuck around the outer walls of the abbey, hurried across an open road, ducked into the bushes, and followed a stream. Not far upriver stood the abandoned millhouse Tuck had described.

"He wasn't kidding," Willa murmured. "It does look like it could be blown over by a sneeze."

I opened the door an inch at a time, lest the roof fall in.

It didn't, though I made sure to stifle the sneeze set off by the dust. Clearly, the place hadn't been used in years. The waterwheel still turned, powered by the stream, creating a constant rumble outside the west wall. The inner mechanism had been disengaged, letting the massive millstone slumber.

That was the creek side of the room. A nook on the far side had been set up to meet a miller's basic needs, with a small table, washbasin, bed, and hearth.

Willa toed the dusty woodpile. "Well, it's drier than I am."

Tuck reappeared soon after with a bundle of supplies.

"Extra-large for you." He tossed a tunic at me and another at Willa. "Small for you..."

She caught it with one hand, growling, "I'm not small."

"Medium, I mean." Tuck's lips curled.

Willa shot him a look, then held it up to her body for size.

"I know it's not the height of fashion, but that's what we have," Tuck said. "The sooner we get you out of your clothes, the better."

She stuck her hands on her hips. "I beg your pardon?"

I love it when she's fierce, my bear murmured.

I had to admit, I did too. But mostly when that ferocity wasn't aimed at me.

Tuck stuck up his hands. "Not what I meant." Then he sighed. "Or maybe I did. I've been here so long, I'm going crazy. Sorry."

Lucky for him, Willa let that slide.

"Anyway, you need to get dry and warm." Tuck thumped a loaf of bread and some cheese onto the table, then tossed a couple of blankets onto the narrow bed. "That's the best I could do right now. There's enough mist around that you can make a fire, but keep it small."

"This is great. Thank you," Willa said.

"My pleasure," Tuck replied. "I'll check in on you tomorrow. How long are you thinking of sticking around?"

I looked at Willa, who nodded at the question in my eyes. Funny how that form of communication worked more smoothly for us than talking.

"We'll be gone in the morning," I assured Tuck.

He shook his head. "From what I hear, Sir Guy means business. He's got his men combing the countryside for that loot that went missing."

Willa averted her eyes and pinched her lips. An improvement over shooting me a dirty look that said *All your fault,* I supposed.

"They're also on the lookout for two suspicious characters who snuck out of Nottingham before the gates closed. The description is vague, but it's enough. If anyone spots your size — or your hair —" Tuck pointed at Willa "— it's over."

Willa glanced at me as if to say, *Told you you're too big.*

I shrugged, tempted to retort, *Told you your hair is too beautiful.*

Except, oops. I'd only ever thought that part. That, and other things I would never utter like, *Could I run my fingers through it just one time?*

And that was just the start of a catalogue of wishes I'd dreamed of during my nap. Wishes like seeing her long, fiery locks spread out over a pillow as she looked up at me, both of us naked and in bed. Wishes like me taking a turn on the pillow while Willow straddled me and bucked, making her silky hair fan the air while her lips moved in wordless ecstasy.

I cleared my throat. Too bad I couldn't do the same with my mind.

"You'd be wise to lie low for a couple of days," Tuck continued. "With the sheriff called out of town, there's no one to stand up to Sir Guy."

I frowned. "What do you know about that? Where did the sheriff go? Why?"

Tuck shrugged, but his normally cheery eyes showed concern. "Apparently, he got called in to assist the sheriff of Darby. That's all I know."

Not good. Robynne hadn't let on, but I knew she was worried. Then again, the sheriff's absence might be a good thing. Sir Guy was a wolf shifter, and if he discovered that Daniel — the sheriff — was a dragon... Not good. A dragon would have the upper hand in a one-on-one fight, but in terms of our broader mission, Daniel's greatest asset was helping us from the inside. We couldn't afford to have him outed as a shifter — or as our ally.

My frown deepened. Was it possible that Sir Guy suspected Daniel and had him called away deliberately? Worse, what if it was an ambush of some kind?

No wonder Robynne had taken the news as a blow.

So many questions. So much hanging in the balance. So little I could do to intervene.

All I could do was chase down the treasure and further our cause that way. The treasure I had let slip away.

All your fault. This time, I was the one muttering at myself.

I glanced at Willa, wishing I could explain.

"All good?" Tuck asked.

I shook myself out of my reverie. "Yes. Sure. Good."

"Peachy." Willa plucked at her wet sleeve.

"Well, I'll check in on you two from time to time."

Tuck's eyes sparkled as he glanced between Willa and me, and his mischievous grin said, *Oh, I'll be checking in on you two, all right.*

Thank goodness bells pealed in the distance just then. Tuck sighed. "I have to go. It's time to pray... again."

"How many times a day?" Willa asked.

Tuck waved in a *Don't ask* gesture. "Too many. Imagine being God. Wouldn't He want a break from time to time?"

Willa chuckled. "You could suggest that to the abbot."

Tuck grinned. "I did. He was not amused. I had to take a vow of silence for a week."

The bells continued tolling, each *bong* pulling poor, reluctant Tuck another step away.

"I have to go," he repeated sadly. "But if trouble appears, I'll be here." The thought seemed to cheer him a bit.

With that, he strode away.

Willa stood at my shoulder in the doorway, watching him go. "No way is that man a priest."

I knew what she meant. Tuck was born — and built — for battlefields, not pews or cloisters.

The lion shifter must have heard, because he turned with a sigh. "Either God hates me, or he really does move in mysterious ways."

He waved, then disappeared, leaving us alone.

Very alone, as I discovered when Willa turned and bumped into me. The moment our bodies touched, fire raced through my veins.

"Sorry," we both said at the same time.

In our rush to part, our feet tangled, and I had to grab her to keep from falling over. That brought her emerald eyes in line with mine, and I went dizzy for a time. I held her for a while like that — too long, I knew, but Willa didn't seem to mind. Her lips moved — replaying our kiss, perhaps? And if so, would she let me kiss her again? Was there any chance a guy like me and a woman like her...

With a gulp, I set her back on her feet and stepped away.

Chapter Ten

WILLA

Being out of the rain for the night was great. The food Tuck had left us was simple but good, especially after such a cold, dreary day. Having a place to shelter while avoiding Sir Guy's forces was great too.

The only thing not great that evening was me.

The shiver that had come and gone throughout the day stopped for a while, then came back with a vengeance. Holding my hands over the tiny fire John made didn't help, and neither did standing close to it — so close that John yanked me back and clapped out the flame at the hem of my tunic.

"Be careful," he admonished. "Are you all right?"

"Just a little cold," I muttered, rubbing my arms.

I tugged off my boots, then set the spelled dagger beside the bed, along with the rest of my weapons — a short knife, my double-edged Quillon dagger, a long knife, then my baselard with its H-shaped hilt...

One by one, I banged them onto the table, and John's eyebrows jumped every time.

How many weapons does one woman need? his startled expression asked.

I was so tired, I didn't bother uttering the answer. *One more than her enemies expect.*

There was only one bed, and normally, I would have put up a fight over who got it — or who didn't, because God forbid one of us become indebted to the other by claiming comfortable digs for the night.

But I was shaking so hard by then, I flopped down without a word of protest, clutching the blanket tightly. After another long minute of shivering, I wrapped the edges closer to my body, pulled a corner over my head, and hunkered down in darkness.

"Are you all right?" John asked from outside that cocoon.

"Fine." My teeth chattered.

Silence reigned. Then a floorboard creaked — John stepping closer.

"Really fine?"

"Really," I lied. The last thing I wanted was help. Especially *his* help.

I clasped my hands at my chest, desperate to retain every scrap of heat.

More silence ensued, though that didn't last long either. Something rustled, followed by something soft and light settling over me. Despite having my eyes squeezed shut and facing the wall, I knew it was John covering me with his blanket.

"You can't give me yours," I tried weakly.

"I can. I did."

If I'd had energy for anything besides shivering, I would have refused. But the extra bit of warmth was an irresistible drug pulling me closer to oblivion.

Ever so gently, he tucked in the edges of the blanket, wrapping me like a mummy.

"How's that?"

"Better. Thanks," I said between shivers. "How is it that you're not cold?"

"We're pretty tough," he murmured.

I wanted to snort. I was tough too. As tough as they came. And yet all I could do was lie there, shaking like a terrified rabbit. God, I hated being pathetic.

My thoughts jumped sideways, and I wondered who his *we* was. The Merry Men of Sherwood Forest? They had to be tough, but still. The only creatures capable of spending a day as wet as ours without falling sick were thick-furred animals. Wolves. . . badgers. . . bears. . .

My foggy mind decided *bear* fit John most closely. He was that big, that capable of *ferocious*, yet still gentle.

Touchingly gentle, like now, as he folded the edge of his blanket over my icy feet.

"Thanks," I remembered to say. "That's better."

Only a little, actually, but I needed him to leave me alone. Nothing personal, really. It was just that I didn't like to rely on anyone. I was fine on my own. Alone was safer. Better. Less complicated. It also meant being lonely, but hey. The trade-off was worth it... most of the time.

"You're still shaking," he rumbled a minute later.

I was also losing feeling in my fingers, but he didn't need to know that.

"It's the way the firelight flickers," I tried as uncontrollable shivers racked my body.

"Not the firelight," John muttered.

No, it wasn't, but if he pretended as hard as I did...

The more I shook, the harder it was to think straight. If only I had that ring my mistress had mentioned.

"The ring of what?" John asked.

"Aquitaine," I said through chattering teeth. "A ring that gives its bearer extraordinary powers — if you believe in such things. It must be with the treasure in Nottingham."

Every word was punctuated by shakes, and it was only after I'd uttered them that I remembered it was supposed to be secret.

And, darn. Now that the words were coming, they refused to stop. "It only works for women, though."

That meant it wasn't so bad to tell John, right? I sensed a gap in my logic, but I couldn't tell exactly how.

John put a hand to my forehead the way my mother had when I was young. It felt nice to be taken care of for a change. But, wait. I shouldn't want to be taken care of, right? And, shoot. Had I really mentioned the ring aloud?

"Don't tell anyone," I hissed, just in case.

He didn't seem to be listening, though. Which was annoying, but handy in this case.

Finally finished checking my temperature, he tsked quietly, and I wondered if that was good or bad. Then he sat in the remaining free space on the bed — the spot where my legs would be if I weren't tucked into a tight fetal position. The bed dipped under his weight, and alarms went off in my mind.

Well, alarms *should* have gone off, but they didn't. Not with comforting warmth there for the taking.

"Don't take this the wrong way..." he warned, sliding into bed beside me.

Clearly, the chill had reached my brain, because the opposite was true.

Just right, every cold-racked corner of my body sighed.

He eased in so carefully and gradually, it was impossible not to trust him. He tucked his head over mine and bent his legs, wrapping his big body around mine.

And, wow, it felt like downing a warm drink spiked with alcohol — the kind that warmed you from the inside. Still, it wasn't just the warmth, but that feeling of *rightness* too.

"You're making it hard to hate you," I eventually murmured.

"Um...sorry?"

God, he was sweet. A good thing the blanket hid my smile from him.

"Just kidding," I murmured.

My shivers were like a long night of rain — I didn't notice when they petered out, but eventually, they did. One by one, my muscles relaxed, and the energy that had drained away slowly returned.

John's stiffness faded too, and he stretched out more comfortably. The bed was narrow and he was big, but somehow, we fit perfectly.

"You know, you're not so bossy when you're like this," he murmured.

I stuck an elbow into his ribs — gently. "Don't ruin this."

He laughed, a sound in the same category as the crackling fire. Homey. Comforting. Warm.

I soaked in the sound the way I soaked in his body heat, feeling slightly more alive again.

"Why are you being so nice to me?" I couldn't help asking.

He shrugged, taking a long time to answer. So long, I wondered if what he finally said was the truth or a cover-up.

Because I like you, I found myself longing to hear.

I bit my lip. I'd held a grudge, assaulted him with snippy comments, and generally been bitchy. Why on earth would this man like me?

And, shoot. Why did I care that he did?

"Because Robynne would have wanted me to," he finally replied.

"Oh. Very loyal of you." I meant it, too.

John shifted his weight, trying to get more comfortable. Which worked — for both of us. So comfortable, I didn't realize that his arm was slung loosely over my side. Did he?

"Is loyalty a bad thing?" he murmured from over my shoulder.

"It's not a *smart* thing. You can't count on other people."

"I can count on Robynne."

His words were so even, so self-evident, I envied her.

"It took some time for me to realize that, but now, I know," he finished.

I suppose he had a point there — and maybe a deeper lesson for me. Trust didn't spring up overnight. It developed gradually, especially after shared challenges.

The thought started moving in a dangerous direction, so I stared at the wall before me, trying to clear my mind. The only other thing in my field of vision was John's hand — the scarred one. I opened my mouth, burning to ask about it, then closed it again. That wasn't any of my business.

"How did you meet Robynne?" I finally ventured.

"She found us. I was already in Sherwood Forest with the others."

"Oh." I didn't pry into the details. Robynne's band were all outlaws, but that didn't bother me — not in these difficult times, when desperation drove too many people to petty crimes and when poor policing charged completely innocent souls.

"Theft," John said flatly.

My eyes went wide, more at the admission than the crime itself. And I was even more surprised when he went on.

"I came across two women with a broken wagon," he murmured. "An older woman, her daughter, and the daughter's young children."

His slow, wavering tone told me these were details he didn't share often. I held my breath, waiting for him to go on.

"I was fixing the wheel for them when some soldiers came along and searched the wagon. They found four golden goblets that matched the description of those stolen from a nearby church." He shook his head, muttering, "Who steals from a church?"

I frowned. Not John. I would bet my life on it.

"The women acted shocked and pinned it on me. Me, who'd offered to help them! They said I must have hidden the goblets there." Every muscle in his body — and there were lots of them, all XXL — tensed. "You should have seen them crying and begging the soldiers. Of course, the soldiers believed them..."

All my life, I'd fumed at the disadvantages women faced. I'd never really considered the advantages, like presumed innocence.

"I took off, but the soldiers followed," John went on. "Afterward, I heard the soldiers claimed I'd nearly killed them, even though I'd been careful not to leave more than a few bruises. What really stung, though, was finding out the church let the women keep two goblets for helping recover stolen property."

I gaped. "That's so wrong."

John shrugged. "That's the way it is. I don't regret that it brought me to Sherwood Forest, though."

I frowned. Maybe, but that ought to have been his choice, not a necessity.

"Sorry. I didn't mean to pry."

He studied me, then flashed a weak smile. "I'll put it down to your mind not being completely clear right now."

I hated being in such a state, but I appreciated his charitable thinking. Maybe it was time for me to give him the same courtesy.

"Are you warmer, at least?" he asked.

Yes, especially my heart, busy swelling to twice its usual size. In the past hours, John had shown nothing but patience and kindness — the same qualities that had gotten him into trouble with those women, drat them.

"Much warmer," I whispered. "And sorry again."

"About what?"

I motioned vaguely, imagining all my mistakes etched into that wall for generations to see.

"Sorry for blaming you. Sorry for being childish. And thank you for helping me."

There. An apology. An actual apology. I was proud of myself.

I sensed him smile. "You're welcome. Thanks for helping me too."

I took a deep breath, plunging into foreign territory. "Maybe we can put it behind us and...you know, help each other accomplish what we set out to do. Without keeping a running tally, I mean."

I turned to face him and, oops. Now that my mind was a little clearer, I realized how close we were. Face-to-face. In bed. Lips mere inches from each other...

Or maybe my mind wasn't so clear, because I swore his honey-gold eyes were glowing. Swirling, even.

"Good plan. Cooperating." His voice was all husky. "No strings attached. In either direction."

Maybe we can attach a few strings, a sultry voice deep inside me urged.

Maybe that was my problem — keeping everyone at a distance. Never trusting.

Slowly, John moved his hand until he was cupping my face. My heart pounded as I recalled our kiss. Even for a faked kiss, it had been a doozy. What would the genuine deal feel like?

He traced the line of my jaw. Was he thinking the same thing?

The candles Tuck had left flickered all around us, imitating the fire in the hearth. I forced my eyes to stay on John's, not go all droopy with desire. But that was tricky, because desire, once kindled, didn't just fizzle away. It simply shifted elsewhere, like down my body, all the way to my core. Close to where I could loop a leg over his and press my body closer...

A good thing those blankets bound me like a mummy.

I opened my lips, just a crack, waiting. Hoping.

John's eyes fell there, and I could sense him warring with himself. Then his Adam's apple bobbed, and he backed away a single, reluctant inch.

"Good plan," he repeated, a little awkwardly.

There'd been a kiss in the making, for sure. But now, it fluttered away like a butterfly. Or rather, a moth. That was more fitting, given the state of those blankets.

I rolled back to face the wall, but my body remained snuggled with his.

"Good night," I whispered.

As before, he looped his hand over my side, and this time, I gripped it.

"Good night," he rumbled, settling in comfortably.

Chapter Eleven

JOHN

That night, I slept on an angel's cloud. Everything felt light, happy, even floating, with cares pushed far, far away. The best night of sleep I'd had in a long, long time.

Waking up ought to have been a misery, but it wasn't, because my arms were curled around Willa, rising and falling with each soft breath she took.

My chest rose and fell too. Hell, I could get used to this.

We'd even managed to hold a civil conversation the previous night, and this morning, I was optimistic that we would be on better footing.

Not footing, my bear joked happily. *Bedding.*

I swallowed hard at that. We hadn't spent the night together in that sense, yet it felt more intimate than nights I'd spent naked — er, frisky — with other women. Not that there had been many — certainly not as many as Robert and some of the others boasted about.

My bear sighed as I held Willa tighter. *The real thing.*

I let out a long breath, trying not to get carried away. Last night, Willa had been vulnerable. I ought to brace myself for her to awake with her usual sass and attitude.

My bear grinned. *That's what I like about her. One of many things.*

She woke a good hour later, stretching sleepily in my arms. Then she tensed, marking a moment of realization. I could practically hear her screech and feel her foot slam into my groin.

But neither came. Willa stayed stiff a minute longer, then relaxed back into my embrace.

Inside, my bear cheered wildly. Outside, I stayed very, very still, terrified of spoiling the moment.

Eventually, she let out a loud yawn that said, *I'm officially waking up now, so I hope you're decent back there.* An exaggerated* *stretch sent the same message, in case I was that sleepy — or stupid. Then she sat up and flicked her fingers as if testing for frostbite.

I nearly asked, *Doing better?* but Willa would hate that reminder of her vulnerability. So I went for a more neutral "Good morning" and tried to find a manly way to slide away.

Willa saved us both an awkward moment by exiting the bed smoothly from the foot end. The blankets were still wrapped tight around her, but she wiggled them away — an action that only made my groin harder.

"Good morning," she murmured, stretching high.

My throat went dry. The light shift she wore was thin, revealing the slight curve of her hips... her breasts... the points of her nipples...

I stared, then yanked my gaze away.

She threw a tunic over the shift — too bad — then finger-combed her long hair and worked it into a new arrangement. I watched, fascinated. Every subtle movement made the dim light catch her red hair in a different manner, and it shone like sunlight glinting over a river. The cascading movements were similar too, right down to the way she formed three sections and plaited them.

I watched, fascinated. Was that difficult or easy? Might she let me try it someday? Or maybe I could start with undoing the braid...

"Now then..." she murmured, looking up.

The previous night, we'd hung our clothes to dry over the open beams of the millhouse, and Willa jumped up to snatch at hers now.

Most people — and all bears — woke slowly. But Willa was already hopping around, ready to race into the day. She always operated at high speed — except at exceptional times like the previous evening.

If I really wanted to rile her, I would remind her of it.

I decided it was safer not to. After all, she still had that spelled dagger.

I pulled her cloak down in one easy motion. "Here you go."

Then I froze. Oops. That would definitely rile her up.

Indeed, she frowned and packed a dozen words into one hard look that said, *I can damn well get my own cloak, you know.*

I stood still, bracing myself for a lecture on how not-short she was.

Luckily, she just rolled her eyes and gave me a tight-lipped "Thank you." Then she tested the cloth and sighed.

"Dry?" I asked.

She shook her head. "Semi."

I hid a grin.

Seconds ticked by slowly. Willa looked up at the rafters. I looked at my feet. Silence reigned but for the constant rumble of the mill wheel outside the walls.

Finally, she thrust the cloak at me. "Will you put it back, please?"

I made sure not to show any emotion. "Of course."

My cloak was still damp too, so I left it hanging. Willa threw a blanket around her shoulders like a cape, throwing me a begrudging look. "Do you never get cold?"

I shrugged. "Not usually."

She checked her boots next, muttering, "It's like you have a layer of fur or something."

I gulped, wishing I could say, *Or something.*

Metallic zings sounded as Willa sorted through her cache of weapons. I counted them with my eyes. Three knives, two daggers, and two extra-small blades that could be tucked up a sleeve or slipped into a boot. She concealed them as deftly as she'd done her hair — and that, wearing nothing but a shift, a tunic, and a blanket. How the heck did she do it?

Afterward, she moved to the pantry and sorted through the slim pickings. "Hmm. Bread for breakfast, I guess."

When we sat at opposite sides of the too-small table, I kept my legs tucked close. It was a battle to keep them there, though. They kept sneaking forward as if last night's cuddle was our new normal.

Willa weighed the bread in her hands before tearing it in two and handing me a piece.

I shook my head. "That's more than half."

"You're bigger. You should get more. You know, to...um..." She gestured vaguely.

My bear perked its ears, eagerly awaiting something like, *To maintain all that muscle.*

"...to avoid starving away to nothing."

I swallowed a sigh.

When she took a bite, her brow furrowed in thought. "Now we just need to figure out a way to get the treasure back. Once we do, I'll be on my way."

My heart slowed to a crawl. What was that again?

I gulped, barely holding back a whimpered, *You're leaving?*

As a bear, I could hunker down for days on end. Time enough to get to know Willa. Maybe even time enough to explain myself and imagine a future together. But Willa was a restless soul, always moving, thinking, planning. What made me think she might want to linger with a man like me?

I forced a businesslike nod. "Of course."

Willa's eyes met mine, and for the space of a heartbeat, I thought I saw a sad flicker. My legs twitched, begging to intertwine with hers under the table.

Tell me you don't feel what I do. In my mind, I practiced a speech I had no hope of ever uttering. *Tell me this connection I sense isn't destiny, and I'll let you go without argument. But if you feel what I feel...*

The fire in the hearth had burned away to nothing, yet I swore I could still hear it crackling. And that charged, tingling heat that filled the space between us — that was only a memory. Wasn't it?

Pinpoints of light shone in Willa's eyes, and my imagination turned her into a shifter. A lynx, maybe, capable of creeping through the forest with grace and energy. Or a deer with big, shiny eyes and a wary countenance, ready to bound to safety.

A bear, my animal side whispered.

My heart thumped. If Willa were a shifter, that would change everything.

Her lips moved, and I leaned forward, holding my breath.

Then a creak sounded outside. Willa turned, and whatever she was about to say was lost forever.

"Maybe Tuck has brought us something fresh for breakfast." She moved toward the door.

My nostrils flared as my bear tested the air. I threw out a hand to stop Willa at the very moment she froze, coming to the same realization I did.

There weren't just two feet out there. There were four. Six... maybe more.

Our eyes met, exchanging a silent message. *Not Tuck. Soldiers?*

I grabbed my staff and stood beside the hinge side of the door. Without a sound, Willa took up position on the other side, one hand on the weapon concealed at her side.

Then someone banged on the door. "Open up by order of Sir Guy."

Willa's face went sour, and I could read the retort in her mind. *I don't follow that monster's orders.*

Monster. Shifter. My bear mourned, and I wished I could explain. *Being a shifter doesn't make you a monster. For every bad apple, there are a dozen good citizens.*

More creaks sounded, indicating an entire unit of soldiers. I signaled for Willa to step back while calculating how to take out the most enemies and how best to protect her.

But her eyes sparkled, saying she had a better plan. I groaned, certain I wasn't going to like it, nor have much choice.

Before I could protest, she checked her tunic, stuck on a smile, and opened the door casually.

"Good morning. What can I do for you?"

Every muscle tensed as I stayed out of sight behind the door. Rage built inside me — a foreign kind of rage that bubbled like a witch's cauldron. Rage that said, *One step closer to my mate, and I will kill every one of you.*

My fingernails ached as my bear fought to release its claws, and my skin prickled in a precursor to the change to fur. I gritted my teeth, barely restraining my inner beast.

"Sorry to bother you, ma'am, but we're under orders to search for suspicious characters in the area," the soldier said.

Willa slapped a hand to her heart. "My goodness, how frightening."

Ha. As if anything scared her.

"A good thing we haven't seen anyone," she added.

The step creaked as the soldier leaned in. "We?"

I winced, but Willa covered up quickly.

"Yes. Me, my husband, and the children." She hauled me into view, pinning me to the side of her body.

The soldiers looked up — and up, going a little pale. Willa stuck her elbow in my ribs, prompting me to slide an arm across her shoulders.

"Just a couple of visitors, honey," she purred, slipping her arm around my waist.

Ninety percent of me was on edge, ready to tear the intruders to pieces. The other ten percent basked in how good it felt to hold and to be held.

"You'll have to excuse my husband. He's a little slow this morning. Well, every morning."

I squeezed her shoulder in retribution, turning her chuckle into a squeak.

Then she rubbed her eyes. "I swear, neither of us got a wink of sleep last night. The twins were up for hours."

My eyes went wide. Twins?

"I know how it is," the closest soldier said, the way only a weary father could.

A second guard peered at the roof, then into the millhouse. "And you live here?"

I held my breath. How was Willa going to talk her way out of that one? The millhouse was far too dilapidated for a family dwelling.

Willa laughed in a way guaranteed to make him think twice about asking more questions, given how stupid his first try was. "Certainly not. We were on our way to relatives in Winthrop, but this weather held us up." She waved around. "We haven't seen anything suspicious, but you're welcome to come in."

I gripped the edge of the door so hard, it was a wonder the wood didn't splinter. Was she crazy?

But once Willa was committed to a line of attack, she was a bulldog. "Just keep your voices down, please. I'd hate to wake the children. Lucy is such a light sleeper. Harold, not so much, but once he's disturbed, he screams and screams."

The closest soldier winced.

"Yes, it's been nothing but crying this past fortnight," Willa lamented. "I hope it's only teething. God forbid it's the pox..."

Every soldier who'd been pressing in toward the door jumped back, and their leader paled.

"The pox?"

Willa stuck her hands up. "It's probably just teething. I suppose I'm just an anxious mother after what happened last year..."

She trailed off again, letting the seeds of doubt sprout on fertile territory.

"What happened last year?" one of the soldiers murmured.

Another kicked him as if to say, *Don't you know, you idiot?*

The thing was, nothing remarkable had happened last year. But Willa's tone had a way of inviting every man to fill in the blanks with all the horrors in his imagination. Even I pictured the worst. The black plague. Smallpox. Devilry...

Willa twisted her hands, the very picture of maternal anxiety. "Just when I think Harold's diarrhea will clear up, it gets worse." Then she shook her head. "Sorry, I'm babbling. Please, come in. We've cleaned up his mess — well, mostly. I'll put on the kettle..."

The more she motioned the men forward, the more they backed up.

"Not necessary, ma'am," the leader hurried to say. "Sorry to have disturbed you."

Willa waved cheerily. "Not at all. We'll be sure to tell you if we see anything suspicious. Where can we find you?"

She sounded so sweet, so genuine. I made a mental note to be doubly wary in the future.

"Um...just report to someone in the abbey," the soldier called, already ten steps away. "No need to find me personally."

"All right. Good day, gentlemen."

Willa waved goodbye for five full seconds before closing the door.

I blew out a breath, willing my heart rate to settle.

She raised a single eyebrow in question. "What?"

I stared a minute longer, then rumbled, "Twins?"

She broke into laughter. Peals of it, so much that she slapped her leg and held her sides.

I blinked, then found myself hooting alongside her.

Children. Pox. Diarrhea. Ha. The only infectious thing in the millhouse was our laughter. We both rocked back and forth, laughing ourselves silly. And for those few moments, at least, our situation didn't seem so dark or desperate. We had food. We had shelter. We had each other.

I choked a few words out through my laughter. "How old are the twins?"

Willa faked an eye roll. "You can't even remember your own children's birthday?"

I grinned. "It seems to have slipped my mind. Like the children themselves. Lucy and Harold?"

She laughed, patting my chest in a *there, there* gesture. "Clearly, they get their brains from my side of the family."

Children. Parents. Family. Notions that had never entered my mind suddenly sparkled like golden combs of honey, at least to my bear side.

Okay, maybe my man side too.

We laughed and laughed, and the sounds — one pitched high, the other lower — wound around each other and filled the room like a fresh breeze. Even after the laughter faded, I found myself grinning at Willa, and her grinning at me.

Apparently, Willa had forgotten to scowl. And, oops. Apparently, I had too.

I liked us better this way. Joking, not arguing. Laughing. Cooperating.

Willa poked me. "Just don't go getting any ideas, hotshot."

My cheeks flushed, because that was exactly what I'd been doing.

Still, I did my best to keep a straight face. "Wouldn't dream of it, honey."

Chapter Twelve

WILLA

We were stuck in the millhouse for two more days. When it wasn't pouring rain, Sir Guy's men were out combing the countryside, and we preferred to avoid both.

On the plus side, my clothes had a chance to dry — mostly — and I had time to get to know John better.

On the downside, I hated being cooped up, and I got to know John better. Not good, because too much time spent gazing into those honey-colored eyes made something shift inside me. Worse, playing house was giving me bad ideas about how that kind of life might suit me if I ever found a good man. A man like John. Quiet. Respectful. Thoughtful. Not at all the oaf I'd thought him to be.

But I wasn't a team player. I wasn't a helpless female. I didn't rely on others, and I didn't conform to expectations.

"Everything all right?" John asked.

I whirled away from staring at the waterwheel turning, turning, turning. "Yes. Sure. Absolutely."

He tilted his head but didn't say a word. He did come over to look through the window at the waterwheel with me, however. I barely noticed at first, he was that quiet. But soon, I couldn't *not* notice, because my heart thumped faster as my senses became hyperaware of his presence beside me. And not just aware, but reacting like one of the four core elements thrown into contact with its opposite. Water sizzling against fire. Air whirling earth into a hurricane. Man stirring up woman.

I swallowed hard, forcing myself to step away rather than inching closer. I sat on the bed to polish my weapons. That would reinforce my self-image of invincibility, wouldn't it?

But, yikes. Even then, sensual dreams visited me. Dreams of heavy panting, and not from another close call. Of dancing oh so close, and not exactly in a ballroom. Of bucking wildly, but not on horseback. Of chasing highs that made me cry out in sheer, wild satisfaction.

I cleared my throat and shot a guilty look at John — at the exact moment he did the same.

We'd continued to share the bed — to ward off the night-time cold, no other reason! — and he'd had to make a quick exit on more than one occasion. Usually, that corresponded to the times when my mind was at its dirtiest. We were that in tune, it was scary.

I lifted the spelled dagger, letting dim light glint off it.

"Care to fight?" I asked. We'd taken to sparring now and then to pass the time and keep our skills honed.

"Aye, but not with that blade."

I laughed. "It's only spelled against shifters."

"It's still a blade, and you're much too skilled with it."

A compliment I was happy to accept.

"How is it you're so good with weapons, anyway?" he asked.

I shrugged. "My mother was adamant that my sisters and I knew how to defend ourselves."

I told him about my mother, her business, and the tutors she had found for us, from the aging knight who'd grown to treat me like his own daughter to the cooper who'd done a stint as a yeoman archer, to the blacksmith who liked sparring with battle-axes in his spare time.

John's eyebrows jumped. "Battle-axes?"

"And quarterstaffs, when the mood struck him." Then I chuckled. "Ha — when the mood *struck* him. You get it?"

How sweet of John to laugh at my pun rather than groan. "I get it."

We grinned at each other for a little too long.

I nearly shared more aspects of my training, like the fateful day I'd been chosen as a sparring partner for a local lord's daughter. The lord was a rare man — rich enough to make his daughter a highly sought-after bride *and* loving enough to want her protected from wayward marauders, cruel suitors, or potential abductors. Since it wouldn't be proper for a girl of noble birth to trade blows with a man, I was recruited as her sparring partner. Our first lesson together had left us bruised, battered, and best friends forever.

Now, years later, so much had changed in the world and for us as individuals. But we were still best friends, and I would do anything for her.

That meant protecting her identity, even from John, so I omitted those details.

I cleared my throat. "Well then, what shall it be today — blades or staffs?"

The answer never came, because a knock sounded on the door. John tensed, then relaxed, opening it.

"It's just Tuck."

"Just Tuck?" the young friar protested.

I grinned, happy to greet Tuck with his daily delivery of food, news, and good humor.

"Bread. Sausages. Apples." He thumped them on the table. "You're welcome."

"Thank you," John and I replied like a couple of schoolchildren.

"Ale?" I offered.

"Don't mind if I do."

We sat at the table and touched goblets.

"To new friends," Tuck toasted. "Desperate friends, but I'm not picky. And to a brief respite from the dreariness of my existence."

"You could always join us in Sherwood Forest," John said.

Tuck made a face. "Difficult decision. I prefer the company of outlaws, but the ale here is better." He sighed, plucking at his robe. "I just wasn't born for this."

It was a joke, but not a joke. I pursed my lips. Poor Tuck.

Then he stuck on a smile. "Never mind. I caught some news from Nottingham. Which do you want first: good or bad news?"

"Good," I said.

"Bad," John murmured at exactly the same time.

Tuck grinned and pointed to me. "Ladies first. The good news."

John snorted. "Lady? Her?"

I decided to take that as a compliment.

Tuck chuckled and went on. "The good news: Lady Thornton has left Nottingham."

John blew out his cheeks in relief.

"Is she really as bad as they say?" I asked.

Both men nodded at the same time. "Worse."

Tuck added, "Her carriage kept getting stuck in the mud, so it took her three tries, but she finally made it out."

"Just goes to show what a persistent, dangerous adversary she would be," John murmured.

"Or how desperate the townsfolk were to get rid of her. Normally, they would have given up on the carriage after the first try. But apparently, there were plenty of volunteers to help get her on her way."

We laughed, sipped some ale, then grew somber.

"And the bad news?" John asked.

Tuck leaned back, looking sour. "Sir Guy is still in town, raging about the treasure no one has been able to locate."

"Isn't that good?" I tried.

"Not if he starts torturing innocent people to find out where it is."

I stared glumly at my feet. My mother often said riches were more a curse than a boon. Now, I finally understood what she meant.

"The question is, what does Robynne plan to do next?" Tuck asked.

John shrugged and looked outside. "I don't know. Maybe it's time we headed back to camp to find out."

Or you could think for yourself, I nearly said.

But that would have come out snippy, and I was starting to understand John. Hierarchy was important to him, and Robynne was the boss.

I heaved a little inner sigh. I would love to command that kind of respect. But that meant building relationships — not exactly my strong suit.

"You should stay another night at least," Tuck said. "The countryside is still crawling with soldiers."

I kicked the floor. "Looking for us?"

Tuck made a face. "Looking for clues to the treasure's location. And since a couple of suspicious characters made a quick exit from town shortly after Sir Guy arrived..."

"We weren't even carrying anything!" I protested. "We were just...just..."

My cheeks burned, because I couldn't exactly say *Just kissing*. Tuck's sex-starved mind would latch on to that bone and run, run, run.

"We just walked out," John finished for me.

"Besides, the treasure had been in Nottingham since the previous day," I pointed out. "Anyone could have made off with it."

Tuck smacked us both on the backs. "Well, you're the two they're after. Congratulations."

I was about to retort when it hit me. If Tuck was caught harboring thieves...

I gulped. "Sorry we got you into this."

He scoffed. "A little excitement is just what I need."

He was playing it cool, but the danger was real. To him and to everyone in the abbey.

I considered our close call. "We should leave as soon as possible."

"Tomorrow," Tuck insisted. "I'll wake you right before Lauds. The only people crazy enough to be up at that hour are monks."

He stood to go, leaving us with a last waggle of his eyebrows. "Have fun on your last night in the Millhouse Hotel. Don't do anything I wouldn't do, kids."

I swear, that man could pack more innuendo into a single syllable than an army of sex-starved soldiers could fit into an entire evening around a campfire.

And damn if the notion didn't plant itself deep in my core.

The rest of the day creaked by much like the waterwheel, turning circles without going anywhere. Avoiding John was impossible in that confined space. Tuck's words seemed to have had the same effect on him, because his eyes carried that same heated glow.

I broke away, staring out the window. It was dim, the end of another one of those days that faded away without a proper sunset. Just dreary gray growing dimmer until night settled in for good.

A sigh sounded over my shoulder. "Nights in the forest are better."

It was John, who'd come up behind me so quietly, I hadn't heard. If it had been anyone else, I would have jumped out of my skin and pulled a knife. But with John...

Not a muscle in my body tensed. On the contrary, a sleepy hum set in, the kind a cat made when snoozing in the sun.

"Better how?" I whispered.

He nestled a little closer. "You hear the birds. The leaves. The stream. You're part of it, and it's not just the end of a day. It's the beginning of the night."

"True, but it's hard to see."

He shrugged. "Humans get too hung up on daylight."

Humans. Funny how his tone hinted at a foreign species.

"Some of my best walks are the ones I take alone at night," he went on.

I snorted. "Sounds nice — if you're a man. As a woman, it's not that simple."

"Oh. Right." John murmured, clearly considering that for the first time.

I closed my eyes, imagining what a ramble in the woods would be like at night if I had nothing to fear. If, for example, I were a man like John.

But I didn't want to be him. I liked being myself. So I amended the idea to, what would it be like with a man like John at my side?

Now *that* fantasy had appeal.

"Tell me about one of those walks," I whispered.

"Well, there's one walk along the stream I like..."

John wasn't much of a talker, so I was prepared to fill in a lot of blanks. But the world he whisked me off to was as vivid as my best fantasies.

"...if you look closely in autumn, you'll find berries, very small but very sweet..."

My mouth watered, and my nostrils flared as if I were out there with him.

"...the water gurgles like it's talking to you, and it feels like you might understand if you listen long enough..."

"That sounds nice," I decided.

"It is," he whispered.

Slowly, I blinked my way back to the present. I turned, finding his eyes closed and a wistful expression on his face. The house was silent but for the rumble of the waterwheel and the babbling stream. Primal forces that couldn't be stopped, like the rain...the wind...the pull I felt toward John...

Without thinking, I rolled to my toes and kissed him. An almost out-of-nowhere kiss, but not exactly, because it had been building over the past few days like a storm. The kind you can see coming, though you choose to look the other way. Then, *boom!* The tempest blows in and sweeps you away.

John slid his arms around my waist and moved his lips under mine. Softly, full of hope and yearning. A lot like me.

When I changed the angle slightly, his lips opened, and I pressed closer. Closer...

"Do those forest walks ever lead to a kiss?" I whispered. My hands were around his neck, my chest squeezed against his.

A tiny smile flickered over his lips. "First time."

I nodded slowly, then announced, "Second time," and rose for another kiss.

I found out a lot about John — and myself — in the next heated minutes. How thick his hair was, how easy to clutch.

How softly his beard brushed my cheek. . . my neck. . . my chest. How easily I dropped my defenses in pursuit of what I craved.

I also learned how many different sounds I could make. Tiny squeaks when his hands cupped my breasts. Deeper hums when his hips jammed against mine. Eager whispers as he pulled me to bed. We shed layers as we went, and a sensual haze set in until I found myself pressing him down on the mattress.

The haze had a golden glow to it, like John's eyes. A glow that spiked to all-out fire when I straddled him and sank down, taking him deep. I tipped my head back, rolling my hips. For a while, we danced at that pace, relishing the newness of it all. Then our breaths came harder and faster, and our movements did too. Faster and faster, right up to the edge of release.

We rolled without separating, and when John took the top—

I threw my head back with a sharp cry as he bottomed out inside me. His breaths were jerky as he moved, obeying my tugs on his steely rear. Then his breath caught, and he tensed, arresting us in a moment of sheer ecstasy. My tight grip did the same, and my body shuddered around his.

Rays of light flooded my mind, blinding me as I came — and came and came. When the high ebbed, then rushed back in for an encore, I cried out again. John made a hoarse sound, hanging on.

Eventually, his muscles unwound, one by one, and he flopped back to the narrow bed. Our fingers intertwined the way our bodies had, and his breath warmed my neck.

Going limp under him, slowly catching my breath. . . It felt a little like the walk John had described — the discovery of a beautiful place I never wanted to leave.

I wrapped my arms and legs around him, holding him close, listening to his heart beat in time with mine.

Chapter Thirteen

JOHN

My heart pounded. My body glowed with an inner heat. My bear hummed in glee.

It really was destiny. *Willa* was my destiny.

I rolled to my side, keeping her close. The same position we'd spent the last two nights in, only naked. And what a world of difference those few layers made! Just a bit of cloth, but they might as well have been walls that said, *This woman will never, ever let you in.*

My bear sighed happily. *She let us in, all right.*

It sounded crude, but the beast meant beyond that. Willa had trusted me with a corner of her heart. I held her tightly, praying she wouldn't make me let go.

She didn't, thank goodness. She just heaved a satisfied sigh and wiggled around so her back nestled against my front.

A smile played at my lips. Most of the time, the woman was all bristly and barbed. Who knew she was a hell of a cuddler once she let her guard down?

"Mmm," she hummed, slipping her arms over mine.

Make that, an unabashed cuddler. I was in heaven, and I wanted to stay there.

"Should I make a fire?" I offered sometime later. It was dark, and the night would be cold.

"Feeling plenty warm, thank you." She wiggled her ass, making my cock twitch. "And if we get cold, we can heat up in other ways."

I laughed. It was the kind of thing guys said around the campfire some nights to make up for the lack of female company. I would never share what Willa just said, but it was fun to imagine it. Maybe that would put the interminable jokes about Little John to rest at last.

Little? Ha, my bear rumbled.

Given that train of thought, *heating up* again was only a question of time. Still, there were other pleasures to discover, like kissing her shoulder and tuning in to her hum.

She wrapped her hands around mine and pressed them against her chest, gently stroking my skin. Her movements slowed, and I tensed as she homed in on the scars. It was hard not to, given how puckered the skin was there.

Then she stopped, murmuring, "Sorry. You just reminded me of something."

My heart thumped harder. She was making the connection, and my human side was terrified. My bear, on the other hand...

I want her to know about me. She needs to know.

She did, especially if we really were meant for each other. But telling her now? Here? And hardest of all — how? A man didn't just come out and say, *I'm a bear shifter. One of those monsters you talked about. But don't worry. You and I are destined to be together. Also, the sex was great. Thank you. I'd like a lot more, and a lot more cuddling too.*

Anything I said was bound to come out wrong, so I limited myself to a few words. "Remind you of what?"

A long pause ensued, followed by a shake of her head. "Nothing. It's silly, really."

My heart was pumping so hard by then, I could hear my own pulse in my ears. "What's silly?"

Her thumb stroked the back of my hand as she considered, then finally spoke. I swear, I didn't risk more than one or two shaky breaths the whole time.

"A long time ago, when I was walking in the woods..." she started so quietly, I had to strain to hear.

And boy, did I want to hear.

But she hesitated, then shook her head, and finally murmured, "Never mind. It's silly."

Not silly, I ached to say.

"Anyway..." she announced breezily. "Not important. Not now."

It was important — downright crucial — but she wiggled her rear against my groin again, getting me sidetracked.

Soon, we were touching, kissing, and heating up all over again. At some point, Willa chuckled, turned in my arms, and pointed at my nose. "You, Mr. Little, are a tease."

"A tease, but not so little," I joked. An instant later, heat flooded my cheeks, because that came out more crudely than I intended. "I mean, in general. Not any particular part. I mean..."

Willa laughed so hard, she shook. "I would have to agree. But don't you dare call me small."

Ha. I'd learned that lesson the hard way. She might be...er, *petite* in stature, but not in any other way.

"Am I allowed to call you a perfect fit?" I slid a hand over the curve of her hip. Despite the size difference, we really were a perfect match.

"I'd call *us* the perfect fit." She hooked her leg around mine, opening her core.

"Ha. You, Willa Scarlett, are a temptress."

She made a show of huffing. "Hey! You're the one who lured me into this bed." The words might have been sharp, but her lighthearted tone took the edges off. "I've figured you out, you see."

My eyebrows jumped up. "You have?"

She nodded solemnly. "I have. You're incorrigible. Impossible, yet alluring in a way I can't understand."

"Um...thank you?"

"You're welcome." She stuck a finger against my chest. "But don't let that go to your head. You can also be incredibly annoying — but even then, it comes from the heart."

I smiled. "Words worthy of engraving on my tombstone someday?"

"You could do worse, you know."

For a moment, solemn thoughts threatened to dampen my mood. What might I look back on at the end of my life? Just long, lonely days, or something more meaningful?

Long but not lonely, as long as we have our mate, my bear murmured. *And together, we'll make them meaningful.*

Could we? Would we? I held Willa closer, wondering if I dared take the leap.

"And what might your epitaph be?" I ventured.

She thought for exactly three seconds, then etched quotes in the air. "*She tried her best?*"

I shook my head. "I know you can do better than that."

A smile played around her lips. "Okay, how about, *She was resourceful, independent, and loyal to Richard, our true king, and through her brave deeds, she helped bring peace and order back to the land?*"

"Wow. Ambitious."

Her eyes flashed, showing me it was the truth. Which didn't surprise me one bit.

Then she added a joke. "Do you prefer, *She drove him crazy to the end?*"

I laughed, and she joined in. Before I knew it, we'd worked our way into another laughing fit. The kind that took ages to fade and kept you warm long after it did.

So warm, I took a deep breath and held it, gazing into Willa's emerald eyes.

She drove him crazy to the end implied a long time together. Maybe even a lifetime.

Forever, my bear whispered.

Willa wasn't a shifter and I couldn't read her mind, but I swore her eyes sparkled as she thought the same thing.

I burned to say something, but I feared ruining the moment too. Did Willa feel the same way?

Her lips twitched, but instead of speaking, she leaned in for another kiss. A long, lazy one that could have meant any of a dozen things. But given the way our naked bodies meshed... Well, the kiss quickly chose a direction and ran with it. Our tongues tangled, and Willa bent her knee to the side, inviting me in.

"Yes," she murmured, tilting her head back as I slid my fingers through her folds.

Oh yes, my bear groaned when she wrapped her fingers around my shaft.

My vision went blindingly white, and I nearly succumbed to the urge to plunge in without further ado. But Willa's hands guided my head down...down...down to her most secret place. I happily complied, letting my tongue preview all the wicked things I planned to do to her soon.

I licked her straight into one...two...three orgasms guaranteed to make a woman go limp with satisfaction for the rest of the night. But Willa bounced back shortly after each, demanding more...more...

"More," she groaned, dragging her nails over my back.

It didn't take an astute shifter to catch the hint. I kissed my way north again until I was consuming her mouth. At the same time, her hips sought out mine, and a moment later...

"Yes," Willa breathed when I filled her with my thick shaft. "Yes..."

When she locked her legs around my waist and started rocking, each movement was punctuated by a little whimper of need. The bed joined in with matching creaks that amplified as I met each of her bucks with a thrust. Gradually, we worked our way into a perfect rhythm, then broke into a frenzy of sheer, burning need. My vision went a little blurry, and a bead of sweat slid down my chest, though everything else was pure speed. Finally, I exploded with a grunt matched by Willa's sharp cry. We both froze there, clinging to the high as long as we could. Then we slowly, breathlessly, let loose.

It was a full minute before Willa walked her fingers lazily across my back and sighed. Other than kissing her shoulder, I didn't move. I couldn't. I was too busy thinking about what might come next. A lifetime together, or just one night of sizzling memories?

A lifetime, my bear cast his vote immediately.

Willa's tight embrace hinted at the same thing, and I couldn't help but hope. But hope was a tricky thing, and nights could be filled with illusions. I held her close and shut my eyes, wondering what truth the harsh light of day might bring.

∞∞∞∞

Sometime later, I woke to a sound. Raising my head, I listened, then dismissed it. Just another creak of the waterwheel.

I settled back down on the mattress, nuzzling Willa's shoulder.

Mmm, my bear hummed dreamily.

I tucked the blanket around her and closed my eyes, soaking in the feeling. I'd never minded nights alone, but suddenly, that option seemed miserable. What would I do with the empty space between my arms? What would I sniff if not Willa's honeysuckle scent?

Then I groaned, because nature called, and the only thing that bed didn't offer was a way to take care of that. I lay quietly for a while before giving in and slipping out of bed.

Even then, I stood beside the bed for a while, watching the rise and fall of Willa's chest and the shape of her fingers, still curled around where mine had been. Beautiful, really. The beauty of peace, I supposed. Peace and satisfaction.

My inner bear congratulated himself on a job well done. But I was just as at peace, so maybe I ought to congratulate Willa.

Then I caught myself. Yet again, I was keeping tallies. Did it matter who made whom feel good as long as the result was a peaceful night for us both?

No. Not in a relationship built to last.

Finally, I forced myself away and padded outside. Cool air nipped my naked skin, waking my wild side, and I found myself itching to shift into bear form. It had been several days — too long for any self-respecting bear.

And so, in spite of the siren call of a woman and a warm bed, I shifted and circled the millhouse a few times. It never hurt to check one's surroundings, especially when far from home.

Raindrops dampened my fur as I rambled past bushes and under trees. The ground was rich and moist under my paws. I saw no sign of any recent comings or goings except Tuck. Water gurgled down the creek and splashed from the mill wheel as it turned around and around.

Then a chuff sounded, and I spun around.

The hair on my back flattened into place a moment later. It was Tuck in lion form.

I couldn't sleep, so I figured I'd check the area, he yawned, showing monstrously big teeth. *Same for you?*

I doubted he'd left a bed as warm as mine, but I nodded — and made sure to stay upwind. What happened between Willa and me was private. Precious.

Perfect, my bear threw in another happy hum.

Everything seems quiet, Tuck reported. Then he sighed, lashing his tufted tail. *As always.*

The poor guy needed action so desperately, I almost wished for trouble to appear for his sake.

Any news from Robynne? I asked as we ambled parallel to the river.

Tuck shook his head, making his thick mane bounce. *Alan stopped by, but there's no news. Nothing about the sheriff, nothing about the treasure.*

What if calling the sheriff away was a trap? I wondered aloud.

Tuck's whiskers twitched. *If it is, Robynne will see through it. Besides, you have enough danger to worry about here.*

I peered through the trees to the abbey and surrounding fields. *You're right. We've already had visitors. Still, that was a while ago.*

Tuck whirled. *What?*

I explained the whole encounter, and though Tuck laughed at Willa's solution, he quickly grew somber.

What if they had been shifters? What if they had tried taking Willa?

I growled. *No one takes Willa.*

My vehement tone made Tuck whip his head around, and I did my best to cover up.

No one could take her by force — not even a shifter. Well, not without a fight.

Tuck considered. *I know she's fierce, but how successful would a wee female like her be in a shifter fight?*

I gritted my teeth to keep from growling, *She's not little.*

Instead, I stuck to, *She's more than capable, and carrying a spelled dagger helps too.*

Tuck tilted his head. *Spelled to. . . ?*

Spelled to kill shifters. So watch you don't catch her off guard, I half joked. *There's a special ring too. The Ring of Aquitaine.*

Tuck stared. *She has the Ring of Aquitaine?*

It sounded like he'd heard of it, but how was that possible?

A vague memory poked my mind, and my bear grumbled. *Willa said to keep that secret.*

Oops. Right. Well, it didn't seem as if she actually had it in her possession. But just in case, I covered up.

Or maybe some other ring. It's all the same to me, I said quickly. Too quickly? Tuck's interest was definitely piqued.

Still, he held his tongue, and I left it at that.

We walked a little farther, then paused at a place where the river curved, creating a wide cascade. Not as nice as a waterfall, but pretty all the same.

We should bring Willa here, my bear enthused. *And a picnic. Biscuits and honey. Wouldn't that be nice?*

Yes, it would be. But we'd need better weather first, and more importantly, a safer time.

I pawed the ground. If only multiple lines of trouble hadn't chosen right now to converge.

Destiny, a voice whispered in my mind.

I clenched my teeth, then circled back toward the millhouse, drawn by Willa as powerfully as I'd been drawn by the call to shift. She was just as much a need, an instinct.

Tuck tilted his head to the south. *I'll continue patrolling a little longer. Care to join me?*

I shook my head. I'd only been away a short time, but I was burning to hold Willa again.

When Tuck loped off, I rushed back to the millhouse. Now that the need for Willa had set in, I couldn't shake it off.

Destiny, the rumble of the waterwheel said as I shifted to human form.

I stood outside the door a while, chilly and pensive. Destiny had never occupied me much. But now... Where was it taking me, and could I trust it?

Then I slipped back inside, eager to hold my mate.

Chapter Fourteen

JOHN

"Psst."

I waved away the buzzing mosquito and pulled the blanket over my head. But a moment later...

"Psst."

Now the sound came with a poke, and I unleashed my claws to swipe at whatever that was.

"Whoa." Someone jumped away. "Watch it."

I frowned. Tuck? He wasn't supposed to wake us until later.

I growled, scowling at him. "It can't be Lauds already."

"It isn't. But—"

"Mmm?" Willa murmured, half in sleep.

I smoothed a hand over her shoulder, then froze. That was her naked shoulder, along with her naked everything, all pressed up against naked me. The blankets covered the good bits — mostly — but they couldn't hide the truth.

Tuck grinned. "Sleep well?"

Hell yes. Like the best, weeklong winter slumbers my bear loved to take, but better. Sleep like heaven — and dammit, I would still be there if it weren't for Tuck.

My scowl deepened. "What the hell are you doing, sneaking up on us?"

"You mean, banging on the door and stomping over every creaky floorboard to make sure you were decent?"

"Well, we're not," I grumbled, trying to regain some sense of dignity.

But, hell. He was right. Usually, I woke at the slightest sound — or scent. Was I losing my touch?

Willa stirred in my arms, then blinked like a sleepy kitten. When she spotted Tuck, she did a double take.

I held my breath, waiting for my little spitfire to explode. At me. At Tuck. At the world.

But she just yawned and murmured, "Oh. Hi."

Tuck waggled his fingers. "Good morning."

She shook her head. "This is not morning. Come back at first light. Better yet, second light, whenever that is."

Tuck chuckled. "Ha. Second light. Good one." Then he grew more serious. "Sadly, this can't wait. You have to get up right away."

Willa turtled back under the blanket, refusing to budge.

I was sure she was wired the way I was — always tuned in to danger and ready to jump to her feet. The fact that she didn't made my bear puff out his chest in pride.

That's my woman, and I satisfied her. Deeply. Then the beast chuckled. *Deeply. You get it?*

Great. Another crude comedian when all I wanted was sleep.

"Alan just flew in with an urgent message," Tuck persisted. Then he froze at the slip. Alan was an eagle shifter, but Willa didn't know that. Luckily, she was too groggy to catch the *flying* part.

Reluctantly, I slid out of our little love nest, grabbing one of the blankets for decency's sake. I'd hoped not to disturb Willa, but the minute I moved, she reached for me, and when our eyes met...

I swayed on my feet. Her gaze was full of warmth. Acceptance. Love, even. Plus a shine that said, *You're mine, and I'm yours. Forever.*

My heart skipped a beat, and a voice rumbled deep in my soul. *My destined mate.*

If I hadn't been sure before, I was now. And Willa seemed to know it too. Even to accept it, if only subconsciously.

My eyes felt warm — a sure sign they were glowing, but Willa didn't balk. We were both too caught up in that magic spell.

"John," Tuck hissed.

If he'd been half a step closer, I might have shoved him. Instead, I gave Willa one last, longing look and followed him to the door.

"Alan was just here," Tuck whispered. "In a real rush, too, with a message from Robynne. She's leaving for Darby and needs you to take charge in camp until she returns."

It was easy enough to read between the lines — and I knew Alan would have delivered her words verbatim. *Leaving for Darby* meant worried about Daniel, the sheriff. Had it all been a trap set by Sir Guy? And *Take charge until she returns* meant *Keep the men out of trouble*. They had a knack for finding it — in spades — but we couldn't afford that now. Not with Sir Guy in Nottingham, eager to flush us out of the forest.

"Robynne said what?" Willa asked.

I turned to find her a step away, with only a thin blanket covering her body.

It was hardly the time to fill in the details with my imagination, but I couldn't help tracing her perfect curves with my eyes. Curves I'd had my hands on until a few moments before.

I growled, catching Tuck doing the same. Not that I could blame him. Willa had a hell of a body, and Tuck had been in the monastery for a long, long time. But I couldn't resist pushing a territorial growl into his mind.

She's mine.

Tuck dragged his eyes back to Willa's face. "Robynne sent a message. She needs John in Sherwood Forest right away."

Willa's face fell. "Oh."

I tilted my head. Why did she look so glum? We'd been planning to leave anyway.

"All right. We'll be ready in a minute," I said.

Tuck waited by the door, turning his back while we dressed and grabbed our things. At least, I did. Willa was decidedly slower.

"Ready for what?" she asked, clutching the blanket.

"Ready to go to Sherwood Forest." Wasn't it obvious? Orders were orders.

I pulled on my trousers, then my boots, but Willa crossed her arms tightly.

"We need to go to Nottingham and find the ring before Sir Guy does," she insisted. "There's no time to detour to the forest."

There it was again — that damn ring. The one Willa refused to reveal details about. Did she not trust me?

"We'll figure that out later. Robynne said—"

Willa cut in. "Robynne doesn't know about the ring."

"What ring?" Tuck asked.

Willa gave me an accusing look that said, *See what you made me reveal?*

Still, I couldn't afford to budge on this one. "Robynne doesn't know because you didn't tell her." Then I let a hard look fill in the rest. *You didn't even give me more than a few hints. Don't you trust me?*

"Wait. Do you mean the Ring of Aquitaine?" Tuck asked.

Willa's eyes flashed, and my stomach sank. That was supposed to be a secret.

She glared at Tuck. "How do you know about that?"

Tuck's eyes strayed to me, guiding Willa's glare there. Her mouth slowly opened, and her jaw went hard.

"You told him. You told him, didn't you?"

Not a question. An accusation. One I was absolutely guilty of.

I opened my mouth, but no words came out.

"I can't believe you told him," she fumed. "I said not to tell anyone!"

"I...I..." I stammered for a while, but really, what was there to say?

"I won't tell anyone," Tuck swore, trying to calm her down.

But it was too late, and it was about to get worse.

"Wait. When did you even have a chance to talk?" she asked.

Anger was like fire; it ignited everything in its vicinity. Now I was angry too. "I went out for a few minutes last night. Did I need permission from you?"

"No, but you didn't have permission to tell Tuck!"

Now she was yelling. Not good. And when her eyes narrowed in suspicion, I could imagine the words her pinched lips held back.

What other secrets are you keeping from me? Can I trust you at all?

And just like that, the walls we'd let down around each other flew back up.

Tuck patted the air with his hands. "One thing at a time. Right now, you're needed in Sherwood Forest."

Willa shook her head. "The ring is in Nottingham."

"Which is crawling with Sir Guy's men," he pointed out.

"Exactly why we need to find it before they do," she insisted.

"We?" I asked.

Her glare made words superfluous. Words like, *Yes, we. Unless you're cutting out when I need you most.*

I jutted my jaw. Wherever Willa went, I went. It was wired into my soul, like hibernating in winter or wandering the woods at nighttime.

Tuck gave me a hard look. "Robynne needs you. The men need you."

Willa needs us, my bear insisted.

Somehow, I had to convince her. But that was a lot like convincing a brick wall.

"You could split up," Tuck suggested.

I tensed. Willa frowned.

"Or not," Tuck murmured a second later.

Definitely not, my bear grumbled.

"We'll work out a plan," I promised. "As soon as we get back to camp. We'll need help to find that ring anyway."

There. That sounded reasonable, didn't it?

But Willa stood her ground, looking more and more like a goddess of war in that toga-style blanket.

"That will take too long. One or two people can sneak in and out better than an army can."

One or two. I could read between those lines too. *I'll do it without you if I have to,* in other words.

I jerked my head in a no. "One person can't carry the entire loot."

Her eyes blazed as if I'd just called her incapable. And, crap. To Willa, that was like a war whoop.

Her jaw went all hard in a look that said, *I'll show you who's capable.*

"We don't need the whole loot," she insisted. "The ring is everything. It can help Robynne."

I shook my head. "Too risky. It could jeopardize getting the rest of the loot for King Richard's ransom."

"If I find the ring, I'll likely find the whole loot. Then we can make a plan to come back for it."

Tuck stirred the air with his hands. "We don't have time for this."

Willa shot him a dark look, but she did reach for her clothes. Tuck turned away, giving her privacy, and without thinking, I did too. But the moment I did, I felt Willa's glare on my back.

I turned back, but it was too late. Her glare held firm.

I thought we were past that, her expression said. *I thought we trusted each other.*

I kept my eyes locked on hers. *I thought so too.*

Ten hard seconds of glaring later, Willa turned away. She pulled on her clothes and gathered her things deliberately, the way a knight readied himself for battle. Not a good sign.

My chest squeezed, and my inner war raged on. Where did my allegiance lie — with Robynne and the Merry Men, or with the woman I loved?

Then my chest squeezed harder, because what if it wasn't love?

It is. It is! my bear insisted.

I swallowed hard. I'd seen love make fools of good men. Was I no different from them?

Not when it's destiny, my bear cried. *But destiny always comes with tests. We have to prove ourselves.*

I made a face. I'd seen plenty of that in this age of crusading — men marching off to prove themselves. Mostly, they just got themselves killed, leaving behind hungry, grieving families. Real heroes were those who did the responsible thing, resisting the pointless dares destiny threw around.

I tried backtracking. "Robynne said—"

Again, Willa cut me off. "Much as I respect Robynne, you have to think for yourself."

I tried. I really did. But frankly, I'd gotten used to Robynne doing the deep thinking. The best reply I could come up with was, "I have to think of the big picture, not just myself."

And, oops. That didn't come out right.

Willa's eyes narrowed to fiery slits. "Only thinking of myself? You think that's what I'm doing?"

"That's not what I meant. It's just that you have no idea the power you're playing with, especially when it comes to magic."

"And you do?"

I clenched my jaw. Yes, I did. But explaining meant revealing who I was, as well as the truth about the shifters of Sherwood Forest. The risk was too great.

Tuck's tense posture reminded me of exactly that point, drilled into us shifters from our earliest days.

"Please, Willa," I tried. "Come with me to Sherwood Forest. We can think everything over there."

Yes, my bear begged. *Please come with me. Stay with me. Forever.*

"We can think everything over on the way to Nottingham," she insisted.

"Don't be foolhardy."

Her eyes flared. "It's better than being scared or not thinking for yourself."

She emphasized both like cardinal sins right up there with lust, gluttony, and greed.

"You could be hurt. Captured. Maybe even killed."

Willa bristled. "Again, I'm not capable?"

"That's not what I'm saying. But even you can't win against hundred-to-one odds."

She strapped on her dagger defiantly. "So maybe I get hurt. That's an informed decision I'm willing to make."

"If you get hurt, anyone who cares about you gets hurt too."

Like me, my bear added mournfully.

Bells pealed, and the sound carried across the dark, hushed landscape.

"Lauds," Tuck muttered. "I have to go. And so do you." He pointed to me, then turned to Willa and took a deep breath. "Godspeed, Willa. I fear you're heading into a tempest, but I wish you fair winds and following seas."

With that, he was gone. A moment later, Willa and I stepped outside.

I closed the door on all the special moments we'd shared in our unexpected refuge. Tender moments. Vulnerable ones too. And they'd all felt so good.

Click. The door shut, sealing all of that away forever.

I looked north toward Sherwood Forest. Willa faced southeast, toward Nottingham. Neither of us spoke for a while.

"I pictured this differently," she finally whispered.

I let out a faint snort. I had too. But so it went in real life. More *hurt* than *happy ends.* And honestly, I should have known this time would come. Willa had said as much not too long ago.

We need to get the treasure back. Once we do, I'll be on my way.

She took a deep breath, calming a little. "You're being loyal, and I respect that."

Kind enough words, but her expression said, *If only you were loyal to me.*

"I just wish..." She trailed off.

I sighed. I could wish so many things, but wishing never did anyone any good.

Willa patted my shoulder the way parting soldiers did when they hid their emotions. Then she stuck out a hand.

"Thanks for your help."

I hesitated. A handshake felt businesslike, when all I felt was regret.

I took her hand awkwardly, wishing for a hug instead. A kiss. Better yet, an about-face. Did we really have to part?

Tell me you don't feel what I do, I burned to say. *Tell me this connection we have isn't destiny, and I'll let you go. But if you feel what I do, please say so. Say anything but goodbye.*

Willa's throat bobbed, but that was all she said, and my heart folded in on itself.

"Thank you." My voice was all scratchy, because I would never be able to tell her why. She would never know about my bear or that she was the one who'd saved me from the trap or how much I loved her.

All I could get out was a lame, "I guess it's for the best."

A lie, but what could I do other than rush to Sherwood Forest and organize backup? That way, the moment Robynne returned, we could help Willa.

That might be too late, my bear cried.

It already was, at least for the hopes I'd harbored.

Willa nodded not too convincingly. "Yes, I suppose it is for the best. If I find the ring — or the loot — I'll send word to you."

Send word. Not come and tell me herself. This really was goodbye, then.

My bear let out a long, agonized howl.

Willa straightened, stiff as a soldier. "Well, I'm off. You take care."

With that, she strode away, not looking back.

My eyes stung as I watched her thread through the trees. The first hint of dawn colored the horizon in foreboding red and orange that swallowed up Willa's silhouette.

"You take care too," I whispered, while my bear howled inside.

Chapter Fifteen

WILLA

Stubbornness. My mother had scolded me about that a thousand times but always with a twinkle in her eye that said *Attagirl*. Because stubbornness worked. Stubbornness got me through tough times or past people who wanted to keep me down. All my life, stubbornness had served me well.

But now... not so much, maybe.

The rising sun glared at me from straight ahead as I stomped and slipped along the muddy road. I ought to have been formulating a plan, but all I could think about was John.

That oaf. That big, strong, tender, sweet, lovable oaf. Was I a fool to part with him? Yes. Had I treated him badly? Yes. Did I have my reasons? Also yes, though I struggled to remember what they were.

Oh, right — the ring, plus duty to my mistress and to my king.

Funny how much alike John and I turned out to be.

Still, I had to be careful. John had told Tuck about the ring. He'd left the millhouse without a word to me. What other secrets might he be keeping?

Worse, what if his deception went deeper? Had Robynne sent John to stick with me? Was he gathering information for Robynne? They claimed to be loyal to King Richard, but what if they meant to seize the treasure for themselves?

A flock of ravens cawed overhead, blurs of black against a gray sky.

I squared my shoulders and focused straight ahead. I'd been so angry when we parted, my only plan had been to find the ring and head home. Surely my mistress would understand that I'd done my best. But maybe I could still salvage the situation. I could find the ring and the way back into Sherwood Forest, where I could gauge the situation. If I was sure they'd been honest with me, I could patch things up with John. Right?

I hung my head, not at all convinced.

In any case, it all started with the ring, which was probably with the rest of the treasure, all hidden by the sheriff before he left town. The question was, where had he stashed it?

That was just one of several critical questions like, was the ring still mixed in with the rest of the loot? How would I recognize it? Did it really possess magical powers?

I backtracked in my thoughts. If I were the sheriff and only had a short time to hide the loot, where would I put it?

Under my bed, *in the rafters*, and *in the kitchen garden* were all too obvious. Where else, then?

Inside a barrel of wine or pickled pork? Stuck somewhere in an attic? Or maybe, if the sheriff had a touch of class, hidden in plain sight?

Either way, it would have to be an accessible place that others would overlook. Which meant… where exactly?

The question consumed me all the way back to the city, including every evasive detour I took. The rain had finally stopped, and Sir Guy's men were out in force. My disguise helped — a dress plucked from a laundry line and a basket of wool "borrowed" from a barn. I hated stealing from honest folk, but I was sure they would understand if they knew my mission.

Entering the city was a simple matter of sauntering through the north gate, and even my next step — sneaking into the castle — was easy, thanks to my cover story of delivering wool to the housekeeper. I didn't mention the dagger hidden under the wool, nor did I seek out the housekeeper. Instead, I snuck up the servants' stairs to the living quarters, only to find… cobwebs. I turned in circles, studying the dust and sheet-covered furniture. According to my mistress, the sheriff of Nottingham was a cruel, corrupt man who'd taken up residency in the finest rooms in the city. But clearly, no one had lived here for a while.

A pigeon fluttered overhead, underpinning the point. I looked around. Now what?

I was still mulling that over when booted feet sounded on the stairs — lots and lots of boots, stomping along like they meant business. I raced for the opposite door then froze when it flew open, revealing five or six men.

Suffice to say, I put up the fight of my life, but as John had predicted, the odds were against me. Before I knew it, I was dragged to a chamber on the ground level and thrown at the feet of the devil himself — Sir Guy.

"And who is this?" he demanded, sounding bored.

"Housekeeping," I tried.

He was not amused.

"We found her in the living quarters. She matches the description of the wanted woman," one of the guards reported.

I frowned. What description could they possibly be using?

Then it hit me. Beverly. She had probably been interrogated after I'd slipped away with part of the treasure, and I doubted she had the brains to describe me as a big, buxom blonde.

One of the guards pulled the dagger from my basket. No one seemed particularly impressed, but Sir Guy froze. His back went stiff, and his fingers didn't so much as twitch.

Shifter, every nerve in my body warned.

Light glinted off the dagger's blade. Could it sense evil too?

Sir Guy's eyes narrowed as he studied the blade, then me. My heart pounded. My knees were close to wobbling. I'd only ever been close to a shifter once before, when the tax collectors barged into my mother's home and revealed themselves, from pointy wolf fangs to lashing tails. But they were pawns to the cruelest shifter of all — the one glaring at me now. *Really* glaring as if his eyes could bore a hole through me. And heck, maybe they could, given the red glow.

It took everything I had to stare back without shivering.

Sir Guy's silence was worse than harsh words, playing tricks on my mind. He knew exactly who I was, what I was up to, and where I'd been. Or he had no idea but was happy to paint me in the colors of his worst enemy. Perhaps neither was true, and he didn't care. Maybe he was simply running through a menu of torture methods he could try out.

Torture number one: that silence that went on and on.

Torture number two: his pacing, with every step punctuated by the ring of his spurs. *Stomp, stomp, clink. Stomp, stomp, clink. . .*

When he finally spoke, it was a single word.

"Perfect."

The ambiguity frightened me more than a death sentence.

∞∞∞∞

"I don't get it," the man holding my right arm said.

"You don't have to get it," the one gripping my left arm replied. "Just follow orders. Ready? Go."

Together, they forced my hands into two cutouts in a long wooden board, while a third man shoved my head into a third, bigger space. Next, they slapped a matching board in from behind, locking me into the town stocks.

"Watch out," one of them warned while they got to work on my feet. "This little spitfire kicks like a mule."

"I'm not little," I muttered, slamming my toe into his groin.

"Oof!" He bent over double.

The other two were harder to reach, and it was a losing battle anyway. A minute later, my feet were locked up too, and all I could do was glare with as much dignity as I could muster. No easy task, what with my hands, feet, and neck each cuffed into their own slot of the stocks.

Click! One of them secured the contraption with a huge lock. Another slammed my dagger into the wooden frame and left it wobbling there like an oversized arrow.

When the first man stepped back to survey his handiwork, the second man warned him. "Watch out, Edgar."

"Says the man in spitting distance," I muttered.

132

Both jumped back, and one waggled a finger at me. "You can be as fresh as you want, missy. By this time tomorrow, you'll be dead."

If only I had a smartass comeback for that one.

"I still don't understand," his comrade said, wiping the sweat off his brow.

At least there was that. The three of them were sweating more than I was after fighting all the way from the castle to the market square.

A crowd gathered, but their eyes dropped whenever I looked up. I saw sorrow, sympathy, and regret — but not enough defiance to give me any hope of help.

Edgar shot me a dirty look. "It's like Sir Guy says. Let word spread that we've caught Robin Hood, and that will lure his men into town."

The first man frowned. "But Robin Hood is a man."

I rolled my eyes.

"I know that and you know that, but that's the power of rumor," the guard said. "You only need a kernel of truth. Unless, of course, the little lady has decided to change her mind?"

"I'm not little," I spat.

Sir Guy had already tried that tack — promising to release me if I led him to the real Robin Hood and "his" Merry Men. But I would never, ever betray them.

"Come now," Edgar tried one more time. "Are you really willing to trade your life for a few lowly bandits?"

I bared my teeth. "They're neither low nor bandits. They're more noble than you — and more than most lords. And the only laws they're on the wrong side of are those invented by that conniver, Prince John."

Most of the crowd nodded in silent agreement. If only someone would take a stand!

Edger shook his head sadly. "Last chance to save your skin, miss."

I stared straight ahead.

"No? You sure?" Edgar waited a moment, then sighed and turned to the crowd to read the charges against me. "On this day of our Lord 1193, in the name of our ruler, the honorable Prince John..."

I worked up a gob of spit and hurtled it at Edgar's feet.

"...the right honorable Sir Guy of Gisborne does lay down the following sentence to the outlaw Robin Hood." When Edgar pointed to me, everyone in the crowd followed the gesture.

I waggled my fingers cheerily.

"Said outlaw is to be detained in the stocks until dawn, and, in the absence of evidence as to her innocence coming to light, she shall be hanged until dead."

A little gasp went out from the public, and a woman made the sign of the cross.

I snorted. "Is there another kind of hanging?"

A guard gave a little kick while Edgar went on.

"Afterward, your fingers shall be cut off and cast in fire, your bowels burned, your head smitten off, and your body quartered and divided. May God have mercy on your soul."

I sighed. How was it that men could assign gruesome death sentences but leave it to God to have mercy? I was innocent, dammit!

Well...mostly, I supposed.

The guards marched off ceremoniously, leaving me to the whims of the crowd.

I'd been lucky enough to grow up in a civilized town under a fair lord, where the town stocks went largely unused. But stories I'd heard from other places had me expecting rotten tomatoes to fly my way any minute now. Entertainment was hard to come by in squalid towns, and ridiculing a prisoner locked in the town stocks was second only to a good hanging in many people's eyes.

Lucky for me, the only things stirring the air were the furtive whispers of the crowd.

"Damn that Sir Guy..."

"May God have mercy on all our souls if King Richard doesn't return soon..."

"If only the sheriff were here..."

More and more, I was getting the idea the sheriff might not be the monster I'd heard about. Still, with him away, that did me little good.

Then my eye caught on a building across the market square, behind the sympathetic crowd. The stables.

The question that had been spinning through my mind all morning cycled through one more time. *If I were the sheriff and only had a short time to hide the loot, where would I put it?*

I tilted my head, whispering to myself. "In some accessible place, overlooked by others."

I'd never seen the sheriff nor his mount, but I pictured a big man leading a mighty steed out of the stables, then glancing inside with a tiny smile before he thundered out of the city.

I stared at the stable door. . . and stared and stared.

Chapter Sixteen

WILLA

"Hang in there, miss," someone whispered, but I barely heard. "Don't give away Robin Hood. We need him and his good deeds to get by."

I thought of the camp in the woods. I thought of Robynne and her Merry Men. But mostly, I thought of John and what might have been.

Minutes dragged by like hours, with me on display for all to see. I'd never felt so powerless — and the worst was that it might have been avoidable, if only I'd done as John had said.

Stubborn. Impulsive. Overly proud. Each of those was a double-edged sword, and for the first time in my life, I felt the sharp side of each. Plus the soul-deep ache at having parted from a man I might have shared a future with. An honest man — something I became more convinced of with every passing minute.

My head hung lower still.

My mother wasn't wrong about being resourceful, quick-witted, and independent. But I'd discovered it was possible to be all those things and still enjoy the company of a good man. I'd also discovered there was a difference between the kinds of ulterior motives my mother had warned about and the normal give-and-take of a healthy relationship.

Funny how some lessons, you only learned the hard way.

Most people sent me sympathetic looks, but one man came up to touch me where he oughtn't. If one of my hands or even just a foot had been free, his testicles would have paid a heavy price. But I wasn't, and they didn't. Thank goodness an older woman chased him away with a broom before he actually laid a hand on me.

"Shame on you!" she hollered as he ran like a headless chicken. Then she turned to me and whispered gently, "Don't you worry about his type, young miss."

It was sweet of her. Too bad I still had to worry about being hung, drawn, quartered, and so on.

I peeked at the stables from time to time, imagining an especially high haystack. I was sure the treasure was there. It had to be! In one way, that buoyed me, because I'd figured it out. But then I drooped again. The treasure might be just there, but I was locked up here. Well and truly stuck.

More ravens fluttered overhead, cawing. An eagle shrieked, chasing them away, then circled effortlessly in their place.

Ah, to be an eagle and fly away. Or an eel to slip out of these stocks. Better yet, to be a bear and break out, wreaking havoc as I went.

As the afternoon dragged by, a few people worked up the courage to whisper encouragement.

"Don't turn in Robin Hood. Please," one begged. "I don't know where we'd be without him."

"Without *her*," I mumbled, but my mouth was so dry by then, I doubt they heard.

Five minutes later — fifteen? fifty? — a soldier stomped by on his rounds and smirked. "Just turn them in, honey. You know you want to."

I shook my head. How could I ever live with myself if I did?

"They would turn you in, you know."

No, they wouldn't. But after what I'd said to John, I doubted they would come for me either.

I stared at the ground. Maybe being independent wasn't all it was cut out to be. Maybe I ought to try trusting a few friends from time to time.

I pondered that for a while — a long while, because I had nothing else to do. Friends would be nice. Not only to help me escape this mess, but just because. Friends with whom to work toward a greater cause — greater than any one person could ever accomplish alone. Friends to celebrate my accomplishments with and to help celebrate their own.

I clicked my jaw, resigned. A lesson I was learning a little too late. Why was it that wisdom always came after you needed it most?

"Thank you," I whispered hoarsely to a woman who snuck me water.

Others stood in a way to block my eyes from the sun's piercing rays, however briefly, and a few shot me bolstering smiles. Tiny acts of kindness from total strangers that reinforced a lesson I was learning the hard way.

I was also learning something else — how taxing doing nothing could be, especially when shackled to a piece of wood. By early evening, my head hung limply, and all I saw of hushed passersby were their shoes. For a while, I played a mental game, guessing what the matching person might look like. Then I hit a new low, lacking the energy even for that.

When an especially fine, narrow pair of shoes complete with little silk bows appeared before me, I barely noticed — until the person spoke.

"Willa."

It was more of a whisper, really. A soft, worried whisper.

I raised my head and squinted against the setting sun. My neck ached, but my heart jumped into my throat.

"Beverly?"

A good thing my lips were so parched. My voice was a mere squeak, and no one heard.

She shushed me, holding her fan to block her lips when she spoke.

"Oh, Willa. I'm so sorry. Are you all right?"

"Been better. And you?"

"Oh, Willa," Beverly whimpered. Tears started rolling down her cheeks.

Not exactly helpful, but Beverly was Beverly. She wasn't a warrior, a schemer, or a locksmith — a pity, considering my current predicament. She was our mistress's handmaid, more skilled in assembling fashionable outfits than engineering an outlaw's escape.

"Why did you run the day we arrived?" she asked. "Now they suspect you of all kinds of things."

On good grounds, but I didn't bother to explain.

"I had no choice. There was something our mistress didn't want anyone to find."

Luckily, Beverly was more interested in her own woes than mine.

"They've forbidden me to leave the city. They keep asking about the treasure, about our dear mistress, about you..."

A good thing Beverly was too featherbrained to spill any useful information on any of the above.

"Listen," I cut in. "The minute you get a chance, slip away. You need to get home and tell our mistress what happened. Tell her I tried..." My voice cracked.

"Oh, Willa..." Beverly clutched my hands.

It was awkward as hell, what with my arms forced up and my wrists bent down by the stocks. But she meant well.

"I wish I could help somehow," Beverly sniffled.

Yeah, so did I. But honestly, Beverly had never been of much practical use.

Her fan drooped, letting the sun laser in. I squinted, then stared at a glimmer in the light.

And stared and stared.

"If only there was something..." she moped.

I cleared my throat. "Beverly..."

Her lips wobbled miserably. "I know. It's terrible."

"Where did you get that?" I did my best to point at her hand.

She looked at her wrist and brightened. "Oh, you mean this pretty bracelet?"

No, I did not mean the pretty bracelet. I meant the plain silver ring that shone in the sun.

I pointed again. "No, that."

She held up her hand. "Oh, this. Our mistress gave it to me before we left. She said to keep it safe."

My cracked lips parted and stayed that way. Beverly was not the brightest woman, but our mistress was. Bright enough to know about hiding things in plain sight.

I would bet anything that was the Ring of Aquitaine. In fact, I would bet my life.

And, ha. Given the circumstances, that was pretty much the case.

Beverly gave me a *Poor you. You're going crazy* look.

"That." I pointed. "I need that."

Beverly frowned. "What use will this ring do you? It's not even my nicest. Now, this one, on the other hand..." She showcased the faux jewel on the next finger.

It took all the patience I could muster to remain calm. "No, I need that one. I need it, Beverly."

Great. Now I was begging.

Beverly's brow creased. "I don't see how it could be useful."

I wasn't all that sure myself. But I was ready to grasp at any straw within my reach.

"It might not be. But it would make me feel better."

Bewildered as she was, Beverly started to pull off the ring. Then she stopped, showing me the faux jewel once more. "Are you sure you don't want this one? It's much nicer."

Not the sharpest mind, but boy did she have a big heart.

"No, thank you. That other one is more my style."

I stuck out a finger, and Beverly worked the ring on, then hugged me.

I patted her back with one hand, moved by her sweet gesture.

"Go," I whispered. "Go home. Tell our mistress I did our best."

Beverly backed away, dabbing her eyes with a handkerchief. "Godspeed, Willa."

I managed a little smile as she walked away, then let it fade. Godspeed? I wasn't too hopeful.

When the sun glinted off the ring on my hand, my heart rose to my throat. Like Beverly's hug, the snug ring was surprisingly comforting. Still, I wasn't sure what to hope for — or whether to hope at all.

Chapter Seventeen

JOHN

Hours after parting ways with Willa, I stomped into camp and growled orders at everyone. Then I holed up in my den, telling myself I finally had what I wanted — that bossy, infuriating female out of my life.

Then old, toothless Christopher — wanted for stealing a basket of eggs that turned out to be rotten, bless his soul — tootled over, the last person I wanted to see.

"Now, son," he started.

I groaned, because he was about to share one of those pearls of wisdom that made no sense. Things like, *Searching for life's meaning is like searching for a buttercup in July.*

"Go away," I ordered.

He did not obey.

Instead, he ruminated at length about love, life, and how to cook up a hearty stew. I tuned out, but when he finally wound up his soliloquy with *love*, my ears perked.

"Some things aren't worth fighting for," he said. "But a few precious things are. And love is one of them."

It was the first thing he'd uttered that actually made sense, though I wasn't about to admit that. I just growled.

"What if it's not love?"

"Then you wouldn't be pouty and upset."

Christopher tapped my leg and left before I could so much as snarl, *I'm not pouty! And I'm not upset!*

I stared over the treetops and sighed, determined to live blissfully, peacefully alone to the end of my days.

Bliss was waking up with Willa, my bear grumbled. *Peace was holding her. Talking, walking, sleeping with her.* Then the beast sighed. *Okay, maybe talking wasn't always so peaceful. . .*

I thought of the arguments we'd had. The moment I realized I was grinning, I fell back into a scowl. Alone to the end of my days. That was the plan.

Hours later, when everyone settled down for nightfall, an eagle circled camp twice, shrieking in alarm. I ran down to camp to hear Alan's news, which had all the men and dogs stirring — even Nosewise, that oversized canine that had arrived with Willa.

Get rid of the dog. Keep Willa, my bear muttered as everyone gathered around Alan.

The news wasn't about Robynne, as I'd expected, but Willa.

"They've arrested her. She's in the town stocks now, to be hung at first light."

"Willa?" I dropped my charade of not caring and practically shook the details out of Alan.

Afterward, I grabbed my staff and jumped upon a rock. "I need five good men to help me free Willa, right now."

Robert cupped a hand around his ear. "Wait. Did John just ask for help?"

"Well, he is in love," Martin said.

Chuckles broke out from all around, and my cheeks flushed.

Old Christopher shook his head. "It was obvious from day one, son."

I frowned. "What was obvious?"

He waved his hand vaguely. "You and Willa. Destined mates. No use in fighting that."

Robert grinned. "I never thought there was such a thing as cute fighting until I saw you two."

I stomped furiously. "Are you coming or not?"

Martin grinned. "You need to say it again. I'm not sure I heard right."

I bared my teeth. "I need help, dammit. All right?"

"What about Robynne's orders to stay out of trouble?" Robert asked.

"To hell with orders," I declared.

A cheer went up, and I swear, if Robynne had been there, she would have called out the loudest. Our fearless leader had never been one to do things by the book.

With that, I raced out of camp, flanked by more men than I had time to count. At first, I marveled that so many were willing to help, but it gradually dawned on me. The men all liked Willa, and they were loyal to me.

Despite the panic gripping my soul, my heart warmed. Loyalty. Teamwork. Having one another's backs. Who said we outlaws lacked morals?

We ran — or flew, in Alan's case — all the way to the Sentinels, a rock formation half a mile from the city gates. Even in the dark, we could make out their towering silhouettes. There, we huddled together one more time.

Sweat ran down my brow — and not just from running, though that provided a good excuse. My mind spun with ideas, plans, and worries. I took a deep breath, preparing to announce my plan.

Which is... what exactly? my bear asked.

I shushed the beast and issued orders. Yes, it was all a little ad hoc. But, heck. Somehow, it would work.

It has to work, my bear snarled.

Five men would accompany me to the north gate, where two would remain. A third would keep lookout, while the remaining two helped me free Willa. Everyone else would wait in reserve at the Sentinels. According to Alan, guards patrolled Nottingham in a regular route every fifteen minutes, so we would time our entry to give ourselves the maximum time possible.

"Understood?" I looked around.

A dozen heads nodded. "Understood."

Moving stealthily, we advanced toward the gate. It was closed, but entry was a simple matter of Alan flying in, shifting, and lifting the crossbar to open the gate — all under the noses of two snoozing guards. Well, they were snoozing until we slapped gags over their mouths and tied bonds around their hands and legs.

"Keep quiet, and I won't kill you," I hissed.

They cringed, nodding frantically. Either they were mighty cowards, or I was that terrifying.

Alan patted my back. "You're terrifying, even for me. Watch that you don't spook your little spitfire."

I snorted. Nothing frightened Willa. Didn't he know?

And she's not little, my bear growled.

Alan shifted back to eagle form and took off, keeping an eye on things from above. *The patrol is moving away from us, toward the west gate.*

I crept forward with Robert and Martin. The slumped figure in the town stocks broke my heart, and my pace grew faster with every step.

"Willa," I whispered.

Well, I tried. But my heart was all jumpy, and my lips didn't function on the first try.

She stirred and produced a weak squeak of surprise. "John?"

I could have sunk to my knees in relief, because part of me had feared the worst.

"Hi," I managed, trying to figure out where to start. Willa had her pride, and she hated accepting help. That meant the fast way — smashing the lock and carrying her away — was definitely out.

"Um... Would you like some assistance?" I offered as casually as I could.

Like sounded better than *need,* and *assistance* better than *help.* I'd learned by then not to get my hand too close to the dog's fangs, so to speak.

She tugged at her bonds. "I can do it."

Even in the dark, I could see the bruises around her wrists and ankles. But she refused to give up. Hell, if she'd been caught in a bear trap, she would have gnawed off her paw. Anything to get free.

I gulped at that echo of the lowest point of my life.

And just like that, I stopped seeing *stubborn* and saw *brave* instead. Brave and proud. Maybe too proud for her own good.

A little like me.

Robert gave me a look that said, *We're not seriously going to wait until she frees herself, are we?*

I pursed my lips, hoping Willa would come to her senses soon.

"Um..." Robert started.

Willa strained at her bonds, then slumped, glaring at the stocks. A moment of truth, and I knew it. I kept very, very quiet.

A single tear rolled down her cheek, and her voice was a hoarse whisper. "I've been trying all night, but I can't do it. No matter what I try, I can't do it."

My heart ached, seeing her like that. I crouched down beside her.

"Why do you think I brought so many friends?" I tried a little smile. "I'm not enough by a factor of five. But even King Richard took a thousand knights on his crusade, because he knew he couldn't do it alone. Even the best of us needs help sometimes."

Willa glowered at her finger, where a ring glinted. "It didn't work. I was sure it would work..."

She's delirious, my bear said. *Just grab her and go.*

"Willa, we don't have long before the patrol comes through and finds us."

She wiped a teary cheek on her shoulder and glanced up. "Us? There is no *us* here. I'm the fool who got caught."

I knew exactly how she felt, from the anger to the hurt pride and, most of all, the self-reproach.

There could be an us, if you let it, I burned to say.

"Just go. Leave me," she mumbled miserably.

Part of me was tempted, just to prove a point. But then I sighed and kicked the ground. Both of us had been proving our points for so long, we'd lost track of what really counted. Living. Laughing. Loving.

Besides, I knew that was her final scrap of pride hanging on like the last soldier on a field of battle. Stubbornly. Bravely. Fearlessly.

"I figured out where the treasure is, you know," she whispered.

I shrugged. Not a priority.

She narrowed her eyes. "I said, I know where the treasure is. Don't you want to know?"

I shrugged. "I'm not here for the treasure. I'm here for you."

Robert and Martin looked pained, but Alan must have been right about my terrifying expression, because neither dared protest.

Willa narrowed her eyes. "So now I'll be the one who owes you?"

I sighed. Did she have to make things so difficult?

It's about pride, remember? my bear murmured. *Why not let her uphold her rights and principles if she's so attached to them?*

That was the thing, though. Why was she so damned attached to them?

The answer was obvious, though it took me a moment to get it. If Willa didn't stand up for her rights and principles, she wouldn't be Willa. She would be just another resigned, powerless woman in a man's world.

I frowned, wondering for the first time what it would be like to live a day in her shoes. Finally understanding why she didn't jump at the chance to be rescued. Accepting help meant admitting weakness, and Willa couldn't afford that. Surviving in a dangerous, unfair world meant projecting strength at all times.

"Willa..." I started.

She slumped, letting her chin sink to her chest. "I'm being stupid, aren't I?"

Robert rolled his eyes as if he was the clever one.

"Not stupid. You're a fighter, so you fight to the end." I squeezed her shoulder lightly. "But I'd really prefer if this wasn't the end."

She looked up, eyes moist with tears.

The lump in my throat made my voice all raspy. "I don't regret giving up the treasure that day in the forest. I won't regret leaving it behind now. The only thing I regret is letting you go."

Her eyes went wide. "But...why?"

I gulped. Why was it so hard to put a few words together?

"Because I like you," I finally managed, then added quickly, "Even though you drive me crazy."

Willa's lips quirked, and her eyes warmed. When she spoke, her voice was scratchy. "Funny, I like you too. And for the record, you drive me crazy too."

I snorted. *Funny* were the zings that raced around my heart like magic dust sprinkled by a mischievous fairy. *Funny* was that I stood there grinning instead of tossing her over my shoulder and hustling her to freedom.

Of course, now was not the time for *funny*, because any moment now, we could be discovered. But Willa's *damn the consequences* attitude had a way of jumping over to me.

"Wait. It's not that," I said, trying to find better words.

Willa shot me a fierce look. "You *don't* like me?"

My inner beast sighed, lost in love. *She would make a great bear.*

"No, I don't like you. I *love* you. I want you to live with me. To love me. Not because anyone owes anyone, but just because. And I want — I hope — that you want that too."

She stared. My heart thumped wildly. Behind me, Robert sniffled and whispered to Martin, "Aw. So cute."

I wanted to smack him. Willa didn't do cute *or* romantic. Even suggesting such a thing would make her angry.

But after staring a little longer, she only murmured, "Oh."

My heart sank. Was that it?

Thank goodness Willa cleared her throat and went on. "Well, I happened to be thinking the same thing."

Robert scratched his chin. "You love you?"

Willa rolled her eyes. "I love *him*. Even if he is a bit of an oaf."

I beamed, while my inner bear danced around. *She loves me! She loves me!*

The joy lasted for all of ten seconds, when I remembered Willa didn't know about my bear side. Would she still love me then?

My inner beast gulped and went very, very still.

Robert smacked me on the back and motioned to Willa. "As beautiful as this moment is, we need to get out of here."

He was right — first things first.

The problem was, the stocks were secured with the biggest lock I'd ever seen. All we had was my staff, Robert's bow, Martin's sword, and a couple of pocketknives. The sword was too thick to fit the shank, so we tried the knives, but the points broke before the lock did.

"Use that." Willa indicated the dagger stuck into the frame of the stocks.

Robert paled and spoke into my mind. *The dagger that kills shifters? No way.*

I had the same thought, but my mate's life was on the line.

I pulled my sleeve down as a glove and gingerly grasped the handle.

"It's not made of glass, you know," Willa grumbled.

No, but the slightest contact with that blade, and I would be dead. I could sense the magic forged into it. The weapon pulsed with power, like a snake lying in wait, snickering, *I dare you.*

I tightened my grip, pulling the dagger free. Then I slipped it into the keyhole and—

I hadn't even twisted the dagger when the lock shattered. Robert, Martin, and I stared.

That dagger is spelled, all right, Robert muttered into my mind.

And not just against shifters, Martin added warily.

I tossed it aside, then lifted the plank securing Willa in place. The hinge opened with a creak, and Willa crumpled to the ground.

"All good, all good." She tried pushing us away.

Robert huffed. "You remind me of my sister."

I held Willa's arm until she steadied out. Then time jumped, because the next thing I knew, I was holding her, and she was holding me. Holding on like our lives depended on it, and maybe they did.

Mate, my bear murmured again and again. *My destined mate.*

For what seemed like an eternity now, I'd been pushing away my feelings. Now, they all came crashing in on me.

"You all right, big guy?" Robert murmured from what seemed like miles away.

I held Willa tighter, squeezing my eyes shut. Yes, I was all right, because I had my mate in my arms, and she loved me. But no, not really, because she didn't know the full truth about me.

I pulled back, determined to tell her there and then. But Martin tugged on my sleeve, and Robert motioned us toward the gate. "Let's go."

Willa dug in her heels. "What about the treasure?"

I took her arm and headed for the gate. "I guess this is my second chance to let it slip away."

"But—" she protested.

I shook my head. "We've pushed our luck already. And if it's the treasure or you, you win every time."

Willa's eyes shone, and my soul fluttered on angel's wings.

"Robynne is going to kill you," Robert muttered not too helpfully.

Willa flashed a secret smile and whispered, "Oh, I think she might understand."

She wobbled over to pick up the dagger and slid it into her scabbard with a defiant *clang*. Then she took my arm and faced the gate. "Shall we?"

I grinned. I'd been so sure everything would go wrong, but things had gone remarkably smoothly.

Or they had until that point. Then a bugle sounded, followed by the pounding of booted feet.

"Alarm!" someone shouted. "Alarm! Intruders at the north gate!"

"Dammit, I knew that was too good to be true," Willa cursed, rushing me toward the gate.

Chapter Eighteen

WILLA

I ran for the gate, buoyed at having John back at my side.

His words echoed through my mind like a favorite tune. *I love you. I want you to live with me. To love me. Not because anyone owes anyone, but just because. And I want — I hope — that you want that too.*

Best speech ever, especially from a man of few words.

I want it. I want you, I'd murmured again and again when we hugged.

But we had to escape first, and hours in shackles had sapped my strength. The best I could manage was a wobbly, crooked jog. A damn good thing John kept me propped upright.

"Hurry!" Robert yelled from a couple of steps ahead.

I was trying, dammit. It was just that my boots felt like bricks.

Two more men joined us at the gate, making it six of us running for our lives. Behind us, the noise of rushing guards grew louder. Martin glanced back, then cursed.

"Sir Guy's men. At least a dozen."

I forced myself to keep moving, though the forest seemed much too far.

"There — the Sentinels." John indicated a rock formation. An aptly named one, because more men emerged as we approached.

"Willa!" It warmed my heart to have Robynne's men greet me like an old friend. They clapped me on the back and gave me bolstering smiles.

"Get Willa to the forest," John ordered Robert. "We'll hold them off here."

"Oh no, you don't." I drew my weapon.

The men jumped back as if I had cracked a flaming whip.

"It's just a dagger, guys."

"Maybe not just," John muttered.

I didn't have time to ask what he meant, because Martin called out, "They're coming."

The men fanned out, keeping their weapons up and the rocks to their backs. I joined them, standing beside John. He stuck out an elbow and angled his staff.

"Stay back, Willa."

"The hell I will. This is my fault. Besides, these aren't the first men I've fought."

"Not exactly men," John muttered.

I gripped my dagger tightly at that reminder of what we could face. Shifters? I hoped not.

Sir Guy's men faced us, a dozen of them to a dozen of us — at first. Soon, more soldiers joined them until it was two to one. None made a move to attack, however. They surrounded us and waited. For what?

Robert cursed as their ranks parted to make way for another man. One who approached with heavy steps punctuated by the metallic clink of spurs.

Stomp, stomp, clink. Stomp, stomp, clink.

"Sir Guy." John nudged me back with his staff.

Sir Guy's obsidian eyes shone in the dark, and his teeth were a flash of white.

I gulped. Teeth — or fangs?

"Well, well," he said. "It seems our trap has worked. Robin Hood, I presume?"

I nearly whirled to glance behind me. Robynne? She was miles away, in Darby.

And, wait. Why was Sir Guy's evil stare pinned on John?

My jaw dropped, and I was sure John's cracked open too. Him, Robin Hood?

If I hadn't been facing the cruelest shifter in the land, I would have rolled my eyes. Why was it so hard to imagine a woman in that role?

John's hands tightened around his staff, but when he spoke, his voice was even. "That's me."

Robert made a little sound, but Martin kicked his shin.

Sir Guy looked John over slowly, completely ignoring me. I swear, if Robynne had been there aiming an arrow at his nose, he wouldn't have noticed her either. Men!

"I must say, I'm disappointed. I hoped you'd be a more worthy adversary," Sir Guy sniffed.

I wanted to shout, *He's twice the man you'll ever be.* But considering Sir Guy was a shifter, that was already true.

The thing was, John bristled with the same kind of raw power and intensity. Nighttime made it hard to tell, but I swore his beard thickened, and when he spoke, his teeth showed.

"We'll see who's worthy."

He turned his staff in his hands in a slow, measured movement. When his eyes flitted to mine, I swear, his voice echoed in my mind.

Worthy of you, Willa. I swear I will be.

My heart squeezed. How had I ever doubted him? But I didn't need him to fight to prove himself. Worse, he would die fighting, because how could anyone beat a shifter?

My eyes dropped to the blade of my dagger, and I took a deep breath. It was my turn to nudge John aside. This would be up to me.

Still, nudging John was like nudging a cliff. He didn't budge. I doubted he even noticed the pressure. He was too busy staring down Sir Guy. I reached out to touch him, then paused. Now that I was so close... His beard really was thicker, and he was growling — really growling. Moonlight caught in his eyes, making them glow. Not the happy glow I'd imagined when we'd lain in bed. More like the glow of anger about to explode.

"Willa." Someone pulled me back quietly. "Over here."

It was Robert, looking more earnest than I'd ever seen him. I shook him off. I'd never run from a fight before, and I wasn't about to start now. Even if it killed me...literally.

Sir Guy speared his sword into the ground and loosened his collar. "Challenge accepted. May the best man win."

He flashed a cocky grin, then hunched his back and curved his fingers. His face distorted, and his clothes began to tear.

My knees shook. Now, I was definitely tempted to run. Especially when his men followed suit and started to shift too.

That was why we'd escaped Nottingham so easily, I realized. Sir Guy couldn't shift in sight of the townsfolk, but he could out here with no human witnesses.

No one but me.

Well, me, John, and his friends. And boy, did the Merry Men rise to the occasion. No one batted an eye. No one so much as wavered. Had they seen shifters before?

The logical part of my mind got that far. But the rest was screaming for me to run. Especially now that Sir Guy and his men were turning into vicious, snarling beasts.

The three closest were massive wolves. Beside them, a bear rumbled, and a boar tossed its head, showing off long, curved tusks. There was a wolverine too — the biggest I'd ever seen, its lips pulled back to reveal vampire-style teeth — and yet more wolves.

I loved animals. I respected animals. But the creatures before me were in a completely different category.

"Monsters. Demons," I muttered, holding up my dagger.

A huge wolf with obsidian eyes stood at the head of our enemies. Sir Guy?

I'd never been especially religious, but if I'd had a cross, I would have held that up too.

Robert tugged at my sleeve. "This is no place for you."

Up until that moment, I'd considered running. But Robert's words gave me the push I needed to dig in.

I shook him off, angry. "You mean, no place for a woman?"

Robert shook his head. "I mean, no place for a human."

"What about you, then?" I shot back.

I felt a minor zing of triumph, because obviously, my reply had shut him up for good. But when the silence stretched...

Robert looked at Martin. Martin looked at John. John looked so pained, my heart ached. He looked deep into my eyes, willing me to understand.

Understand what? I opened my mouth to ask, then froze.

"Willa..." It was just a whisper, but John's voice was deeper and more growly than before.

I stared at the thick hair on his face and arms. The glow of his eyes. The bulk of his body.

"We're not monsters," John whispered. Then he scowled, glancing at Sir Guy. "Not all of us, anyway."

I stared. Us?

"I love you," John murmured in a frighteningly sad tone. Then his expression hardened, and he turned back to Sir Guy. "This ends tonight."

The dark wolf's eyes glittered, and it snarled gleefully, as if to say, *No,* you *end tonight, Robin Hood.*

Not Robin Hood, I wanted to scream. But I couldn't so much as peep, because John and his friends — my friends — started to transform too.

Martin winced and dropped to all fours. Robert pushed me back, then followed suit. Alan jumped to a boulder and spread his arms as wide as wings. The others hunched, yowled, and snarled while fur engulfed bare skin.

Within seconds, I found myself in the midst of a pack of raging beasts. Robert was a wolf. Martin, a badger. Alan, an eagle who took off with a piercing battle cry. There were another two wolves, a buck with huge antlers, and even a boar. At their head stood John, who'd dropped to all fours, sprouted fur, then emerged as a bear. He rose up on his back legs — and rose and rose, towering above the rest. Honey-colored eyes locked on mine, making my heart go still.

"John?" was all I could peep.

Sir Guy snarled, and the bear — er, John? — roared back.

If I hadn't had a house-sized boulder behind me, I might have run. Instead, I pressed myself against it and stared. The mighty bear raised its front paws and brandished long, terrifying claws. Those on his left were four parallel blades. But those on his right weren't spaced evenly, nor did they form a straight line. The fur around them was patchy and scarred.

John. That really was him. The man I'd been through so much with over the past days. The man I'd slept with, for goodness' sake!

The thought paralyzed me as much as the snarling shifters did.

How — why? — had John deceived me for so long? How could I not have put it all together? The cryptic comments. His mangled hand. His secret forays into the woods. . .

How could you? I wanted to shout at his furry back.

Then I caught myself. John had helped me again and again. He'd kept me warm, safe, and risked his neck to free me. Now, he risked everything again — for me.

That wasn't deceit. That was bravery. Loyalty. Sacrifice.

My heart ached. *Please, no sacrifice. Not for me.*

For another few heartbeats, the beasts growled, paced, and showed their teeth. Then the dark wolf — Sir Guy — barked, and his pack launched an all-out attack. A trio of wolves faced off with John, taking turns to leap forward then retreat. John whirled from side to side, unleashing a series of crushing blows. The enemy boar charged Robert, with the wolverine hot on his heels, emitting blood-curdling shrieks. The buck managed to drive both away, and Robert — a gold-hued wolf — shot it a grateful look.

I pressed back against the boulder, terrified.

A wolf leaped at me, filling my vision with deadly teeth and murderous eyes. For an instant, I stared. Then I snapped out of my stupor, pivoted, and kicked.

The wolf tumbled but recovered with a quick shake. Then he turned back toward me, eyes blazing in anger.

You die, those eyes said, as it closed in for a second time.

I threw up my left arm to block it in a useless, amateur move — one calculated to hide the dagger in my right hand. At the last possible moment, I thrust upward, and the wolf roared, then dropped like a stone. I scrambled back, but the wolf didn't follow. It lay on the ground, eyes open but dim.

My heart beat wildly as I waited. Surely, that was a trick. Surely, one dagger blow wasn't enough to kill such a beast.

I checked, finding the blade smeared with blood. But what really stopped me was the clean part of the blade. It was glowing — *really* glowing, as if lit from inside.

Not lit. Spelled, a corner of my mind said.

I stretched, keeping the dagger at arm's length. Okay, so maybe that *magic* part wasn't just talk.

A theory I had ample opportunity to test when two more wolves barreled in. Thank goodness for the eagle that dove out of the sky, extending its talons with a shriek. The wolves scattered, and the eagle flapped its wings, climbing high again. Then its keen eyes focused elsewhere, and it dove to help John.

Alan. That eagle was Alan. The wolf was Robert, and the bear was John. I went over and over the list in my mind, trying to come to grips with it.

The wolf pair regrouped for a second attack. They were just as ferocious as before, but more cautious, at least as far as my dagger went. Working as a pair, they attacked. I yelped when one raked its claws over my forearm, drawing blood. Then I fought back, slashing and kicking for my life. It all became a blur, until I eventually found myself panting over another lifeless body. The second wolf jumped back, studying me with fearful eyes.

I nearly laughed. I was scaring him? Ha!

The wolf was young and, if not exactly innocent, then inexperienced, I judged. Its tongue lolled as it eyed me, then the others, all locked in their own fights. When it glanced wistfully to the west, it wasn't hard to imagine an overeager young man who'd been lured away from home with empty promises. Then he whimpered — quietly, lest the others hear — and slunk away into the night.

I watched him go, considering. Monster? Demon? Neither really fit. Just another lost soul in a harsh and dangerous world.

Whirling, I focused back on the fight. The tide of battle had drawn everyone away from the rocks. My heart leaped. This was it — my chance to escape!

Moving slowly, then faster, I crept along a faint trail at the base of the boulders. Once I disappeared around the next corner, it would be a simple matter of running for my life.

I sped up, then hesitated. Wait. Running for my life?

Panting, I looked back at the two battling sides.

Sides...

My muddled mind turned the thought around and around. Sir Guy and his men stood for everything I despised: cruel, conniving traitors who conspired against the rightful king, Richard. Facing off against them were John, Robert, Alan, and the other men of Sherwood Forest, who sided with Robynne. With King Richard. With...with...

Me. They sided with me.

A lump formed in my throat. John and the others weren't fighting for Robynne or the king. They were fighting for me. Risking their lives — for me.

Me, me, me.

I stood there, knees shaking, mouth ajar. Then I glanced at the city walls where so many innocent souls slept, ignorant of the shifter fight. Souls who benefited from the *take from the rich, give to the poor* mission Robynne and the Merry Men had dedicated themselves to.

So...monsters? Demons?

Those terms fit Sir Guy, but not John. Not Alan, not Martin, not Robert. And certainly not Robynne, who must be a shifter too. Neither did they describe the young wolf who'd fled.

Not far away, the fight raged on. A fight like none I'd ever seen, yet similar too. Ninety percent of the combatants had been sucked in by forces beyond their control, and often, mere chance determined which side they landed on. Only a tiny fraction was driven by principle, and only a few were corrupt. Even among those exceptions, only a handful stood out — the truly evil, like Sir Guy, and the truly honest, like John.

My shoulders drooped as I watched the massive bear at the head of the fight. Had he deceived me, or had I deceived myself?

I took a deep breath, reminding myself who and what I was — and what I wasn't. I wasn't a coward. I wasn't ungrateful. I didn't like trusting others, but lately, I'd learned I could. And though I made mistakes, I did my best to learn from them. Like now.

Oh, and one more thing. I never, ever ran from a fight.

Curling my lips into a fierce snarl, I charged back into the fray.

Chapter Nineteen

WILLA

I gripped my dagger tightly, knowing it was the key to my survival. At the same time, I had to be careful with it around John and his friends, too.

Shifters. They were all shifters. The thought still boggled my mind. But for now, I resolved to concentrate on Sir Guy and his men.

Dawn nibbled at the horizon, while the moon inched down. I grabbed a rock as a backup weapon, then charged toward the fight.

All the action was concentrated around John — all his allies and all his enemies. Robert and the others did their best to protect John's back while he faced off with the bear and boar fighting for Sir Guy.

I frowned, slowing down. Everyone was clustered over there, but where was Sir Guy?

My finger itched, sending silent alarms through my mind.

A wolf snarled, making me whirl.

Oops. There he was, eyeing me like a sacrificial lamb.

The beast emerged from between two boulders with glittering obsidian eyes, its snarl low and continuous.

Ah, you again, those eyes said dismissively. *Always in the way.*

I kept the dagger unobtrusively by my side, fighting the temptation to brandish it and yell, *Dismiss this, you monster!*

Something dripped from his fangs as he prowled forward. Saliva? Blood? I cringed, praying none of Robynne's men had died in a fight I had set off. Glad, in a way, that she wasn't here, because Sir Guy would use any means to capture her, dead or alive. So, now was my chance to make this more than just a fight for my life. It was a chance to rid Robynne of her worst enemy — and to rid the land of its cruelest overlord.

The fingers of my right hand burned. Had I brushed against stinging nettles? I flicked them, trying to dispel the sensation.

Sir Guy leaped, catching me off guard. I tried using the move that had worked on the other wolf, but Sir Guy pounced so fast, I was hurled to the ground hard. My teeth rattled, and my fingers lost their grip on the dagger. It clattered away in the darkness while wolf paws punched down my torso, pinning me in place for a death bite.

Somewhere not too far away, a bear roared.

John... Part of my soul already mourned for the chance we would never get.

But another part of my soul went into survival mode. I smashed my rock against Sir Guy's head and swayed to my feet. While he staggered, I searched desperately for the dagger. Where was it, dammit? And what was that prickling sensation on my hand? An insect bite — now, of all times?

The wolf growled as it faced me again, eyes glowing, tail twitching. Calculating.

Not a good thing, though I was proud to have earned a little respect at last. Proud, too, to have landed a blow that hard. Harder than I ought to have been capable of, actually.

John bellowed, trying to break away to help me. But he was too far, and his enemies too fierce.

I crouched, preparing for another attack. Wishing I had the dagger because, damn. All I had was that rock.

Or maybe not all, because my finger tingled. Or rather, the ring did. And the tingles didn't just register in my hand — they traveled all the way up my arm. Powerful tingles that said, *Try me, wolf. I dare you.*

I glanced at the ring. Was that what I'd felt? And, wait. Was it glowing?

When I'd been locked in the town stocks, it hadn't done a thing. But now, I felt it awaken.

Every time Sir Guy leaped at me, I warded him off with powerful blows. *Really* powerful, making me marvel at the ring.

The Ring of Aquitaine, my mistress had said. A ring laced with magic I felt intensify with every blow.

Magic that swept me away. I found myself celebrating every hit with a cruel smile. Wielding magic that powerful was reassuring — but frightening too. It was addictive...mighty...seductive, even.

I gulped, imagining the havoc that ring could cause. And not just in the wrong hands, but maybe even my hands. The more I used it, the more I *wanted* to use it.

Die! I wanted to yell in glee. I pictured Sir Guy's men scattering or bowing down to me.

I shook myself before the feeling swept me away entirely. John had been right when he'd warned, *You have no idea the power you're playing with, especially when it comes to magic.*

Another lesson I was learning the hard way.

I staggered away from Sir Guy, panting hard. My foot hit something, and when I looked down, I nearly cheered. The dagger! I snatched it up and held it in front of me.

The dark wolf cocked its head, then broke into a fiendish smile. I curled my hand, terrified that he might have spotted the ring.

But, no. Sir Guy's eyes had strayed from my face to the dagger. The blade glowed in a way the dawn light couldn't explain, and those calculating eyes narrowed with interest.

Now, now. What do we have here?

Wolves couldn't speak, but his eyes communicated every word.

By the way his gaze caressed the blade, he didn't have to ask. I knew he knew.

A dagger spelled to kill shifters could be deadly to him — but also dead useful, like the ring. With them, he could kill John. Alan. Robynne. Hell, he could kill any shifter in the land. And given his power and boundless ambition, they could take him all the way to the top.

I cringed to imagine what that might mean.

For the second time that night, I was tempted to run, because the only thing standing between him and that future was me.

I switched the dagger to my left hand, wiped the sweat off my right, and switched it back again. Sir Guy's eyes followed the weapon the whole time. Measuring. Planning. Calculating.

I did too. How far was John? Was help in the cards, or was I on my own?

When my eyes slid to the bear, Sir Guy pounced. I cried out, falling flat on my back. Then—

Fangs gripped my wrist, and I froze.

I dare you to move, Sir Guy's eyes blazed.

His teeth hadn't broken the skin, but he could sever an artery any time by clamping down. Worse, that was the hand holding the dagger. I was trapped.

Or so I let Sir Guy believe. Yes, he held my right hand in a vise grip. But my left hand. . .

I let rip the hardest left hook of my life. A streak of light zipped across my vision — the ring? — and a crack sounded. My knuckles? His jaw? The howl of pain could have come from either of us, but his grip on my wrist didn't let up, so I still couldn't use the dagger.

Not until John rushed forward, jaws bared.

Sir Guy released me to face him, and when he did—

I scrambled to my feet, raised the dagger, and thrust down hard, channeling the power of the ring. Sir Guy had his back turned, which wasn't exactly sporting of me, but I had no regrets. A man got what he gave.

With a sickening sound, the dagger sliced between his shoulder blades. For a moment, Sir Guy writhed, fighting me, the bear, and death. Then, with a growl of pure hate, he shuddered and went still.

I jumped back, staring at him, then John. Everyone else went still too, and one by one, Sir Guy's men backed away. Only two snarled, loyal to their evil master to the end.

"Look out!" I shouted.

John whirled at the leaping wolf. I rushed to help, but something zipped by my ear first, and the wolf jerked in midair, then fell. Another *something* zipped, and another and another...

"Get down!" somebody yelled.

"Robynne!" another cheered.

Whoosh! A plume of fire burst through the sky. I stared. A dragon?

John, still in bear form, hurried me toward the nearest boulder and formed a wall before me. He was so close and so big, I could barely see. The sky filled with fire and projectiles, putting our last few enemies on the run. But from whom?

John's furry body remained stiff as steel until things quieted down. Then footsteps tapped the ground — human footsteps, to my relief — and a woman's voice broke the silence.

"I leave you guys to your own devices for a few days, and this is what you do?"

My heart leaped. It really was Robynne!

Another burst of fire lit the sky, and everyone ducked — except Robynne, who looked up with a fond smile. Then she spotted me and added casually, "Oh. Hi, Willa."

"Hi," I managed, staring at the circling dragon. Its body was dark, its eyes a brilliant blue, its tail long and narrow.

"Oh, don't worry about him. Just a friend." Robynne winked.

Still, I stared. Don't worry — about a dragon?

I was still looking up when John eased away from his protective stance. By the time I looked over, air shimmered around his body, and his fur thinned. His snout shortened, along with his fangs, and he reared up on two legs.

The process was seamless. Fascinating. It flashed by too quickly to catch every detail, and then John was back. The man, I mean.

I was elated, but John backed away.

Even when I lowered the dagger, his wary stance didn't change. Neither did it when I shoved the ring into my pocket. That was when I realized the thing John was avoiding was *me*.

The extra strength that had buoyed me throughout the fight sapped away.

"You don't want me?" I couldn't help whispering.

And, Lord. My voice was weak, even teary.

Well, of course he didn't. Not after all the other hurtful things I'd said.

I hung my head, certain I'd ruined any chance we might have had.

"Of course I want you," he finally replied. "But you don't want me."

The shame I'd pushed away during the fight came crushing back. I wanted him — desperately. But with shock sitting deep in my veins — not to mention that dragon circling overhead, I could barely speak.

"You're... you're..." I babbled.

"A monster?" John supplied sadly.

I shook my head so fast, it hurt. "No. I didn't understand before, but I do now." I pointed to Sir Guy's lifeless body. "Monsters are those like him. But you... you..." I gulped, then got the rest out. "You're good, through and through. You're a hero. My hero, at least."

The top edge of the sun peeked over the horizon, and his eyes took on a brilliant glow.

"I'm so sorry for everything I said," I went on.

My knees gave out, but John grabbed me before I hit the ground and held me close. Close enough that when I got myself together a moment later, I noticed a... er, detail that had escaped me before. He was naked. Buck naked. An aftereffect of shifting, I supposed.

I dropped my eyes. Robert and a few of the others had shifted too, and I really didn't need to see that. John was plenty.

Plenty, huh? the dirty part of my mind snickered.

In spite of my shock and exhaustion, I couldn't help but sneak a peek. Just a little one. Er — a little peek, I mean. Not a little... um... other thing.

Not little at all, as recent experience in the millhouse had proven. My thoughts went back to that place and time, reliving every tender moment we'd shared.

John, who'd tucked his head over my shoulder in his hug, groaned into my skin.

"And they say men have dirty minds... Do you think of nothing else?"

I grinned as the poke where his groin met my side increased. "Sorry, not sorry, if you know what I mean."

I took his hand, then frowned, staring at it. The scarred one.

My mouth fell open. Those scars...the paw...the bear...

Until then, John's breaths had made my hair stir. Now, he froze.

That cruel, awful trap that day, so long ago. The blood. The agonized bear...

I cupped his hand. "That bear... That trap... That was you?"

He stroked his thumb over my hand. "That was me. And that was you, being my hero that day."

I met his eyes, still gaping. All this time, he hadn't let on. Why?

A stupid question, I realized. Of course he hadn't uttered a word. Not after what I'd said about shifters.

"No one can know about us, Willa," he whispered, sounding pained.

A hard lump filled my throat as I looked at him and the others who'd fought so bravely. Shifters were feared and reviled, as I knew too well. Sometimes, they were hunted and mercilessly killed.

"I understand," I said, though my voice was shaky. "Now, I do. And I'm sorry. So, so sorry for everything—"

He cut me off, taking my hand gently and kissing it. "Nothing to be sorry about. Especially now, because I finally have the chance to thank you. For back then. For now. For everything."

I shook my head. "No, I have to thank you. You saved me."

"Well, you saved me — twice." He flashed a weak grin. "Not that we're keeping track."

I hugged him. "Not keeping track. We help each other just because."

He hugged me tightly, murmuring in my ear, "*Just because is good with me.*"

We held each other for a long time, deaf and blind to the outside world. When the others stirred nearby, I glanced around. All seemed well, so I put my hands on John's shoulders and studied his face.

"What?" he asked.

I ran my thumbs along his jaw. Now, there was just a beard. Moments ago, his whole body had been covered in fur.

"Just wondering where it went."

Worry crept back into his eyes, and he pursed his lips. "Nowhere. My bear is always part of me, and it always will be."

He didn't add, *Can you live with that?* but I could see it on his lips.

I could see something else, too. Something like, *That bear loves you and will always protect you.*

The bear that had battled so ferociously — for me. Yeah, I got that now.

"Always part of you, huh?" I let a beat go by, then grinned. "A damn good thing."

His eyes sparkled. "You think you can live with a shifter?"

"I'll need some time to get used to the idea, but yes — please. If you can live with a human, that is."

He flashed a grin. "As it turns out, they're not all as bad as I thought. Although some do drive me crazy..."

His chuckle was music to my ears. I reeled him in for a hug I held for a long time, while he finished his sentiment.

"...crazy in a good way, I mean."

Chapter Twenty

JOHN

I could have hugged Willa all night — or rather, all day, because the sun had broken over the horizon by then. But I couldn't, because daybreak meant the city would soon be stirring, and what then?

Slowly, I took in the carnage around us.

Robynne waved to the dragon, who soared toward the woods, then dipped out of sight. Then she looked at me, sighed, and looked away again.

"Step one: get dressed. All of you. *Please*," she begged.

We did the best we could with the clothes we'd half shredded in shifting. Robynne, meanwhile, waggled her eyebrows at Willa.

"They look better with clothes on, don't you agree? Although there is one I don't mind glimpsing from time to time..."

Her eyes drifted in the direction of the dragon, while Willa's wandered to me.

"I know what you mean." Willa winked.

My bear rejoiced. *She likes me!*

"Now, then." Robynne scanned our little group. "Is everyone all right?"

There were a few injuries, but none life-threatening, thank goodness.

"We're all good," Alan replied. "Well, except Robert, who took a serious blow to the head. Not that that changes anything..."

Robert swatted him, while Robynne sighed. "Boys, boys." Then she frowned and looked around. Most of Sir Guy's men had slunk off to nurse their wounds, but several lay dead.

Willa's throat bobbed, and her head hung low. "This is all my fault."

Robynne shook her head at Sir Guy's lifeless body. "Well, I doubt anyone in Nottingham will mind. Not when something good has come of this. Still, there will be some who don't agree..."

Everyone went quiet while Robynne thought aloud. "There's bound to be an investigation..."

Willa winced. "I'm so sorry. I didn't mean for any of this to happen."

"Sir Guy had it coming," I growled.

"He did," Robynne agreed. "But—"

Alan cut in, pointing toward the forest. "Someone's coming."

"The sheriff," Martin groaned when a lone figure on horseback drew near.

"Oh God," Willa fretted. "The sheriff? How will we explain this mess?"

Robynne grinned. "Don't worry. We'll think of something."

Everyone watched silently as a tall man rode up on a dappled gray war-horse.

"Hello, Sheriff," Robynne called out.

His eyes sparkled, and he grinned. The horse halted in front of Robynne and snuffled her shoulder like an old friend.

Willa leaned in to whisper to me. "Wait. Won't he arrest her?"

I kept my voice low. "No. See his eyes? Does that blue remind you of anyone?"

Willa's brow knotted. Then her eyes went wide, and she looked toward the spot the dragon had flown to — the same direction the sheriff had appeared from.

"You mean..."

I shushed her, nodding without saying it aloud. Yes. The sheriff and the dragon were one and the same.

She grabbed my arm. "You mean he and Robynne...?"

I put a finger to my lips. I hadn't figured everything out about those two, and maybe I never would. But I knew the sheriff was an ally, not an enemy.

Willa gulped. "Wow."

I chuckled. Yes, *wow* summed things up well.

Startled looks told me most of the others had come to the same realization, but they knew enough not to comment. We couldn't let anyone discover the sheriff was a shifter or that he supported Robynne. The consequences for us all — and the people of Nottingham — would be disastrous.

"Just back from Darby, sir?" Robynne asked all too innocently.

The sheriff's eyes twinkled at her. "Indeed. With a detour on the way back to hunt for that dastardly outlaw Robin Hood."

I hid a smirk. I would bet anything that detour had had him and Robynne wrapped up in a secret love nest somewhere. But hey. Robynne deserved happiness, and she certainly deserved some fun. I just hoped they wouldn't have to carry out their long-distance affair indefinitely.

"You still haven't caught Robin Hood?" she teased.

Daniel, the sheriff, gave an exaggerated sigh. "No sign of him — or her."

Robert stared at him, jaw agape. "Wait a minute. Daniel?"

Then he shuddered, no doubt hit by a mental volley from his sister. I could imagine her hissing in his mind now. *Don't say a word, you got me?*

Robert looked at her, bewildered, but nodded quickly. Having grown up with Robynne, he knew how far back her romance with Daniel went — another secret the good folk of Nottingham must never discover.

"What was that you said?" the sheriff boomed.

Robert gulped, eyes locked on his own feet. "Nothing."

So, whew. The sheriff's true identity was safe a little longer — or as safe as any secret was with Robert.

The mighty gray steed pawed the ground, echoing the warning. Meanwhile, the sheriff took in the carnage and frowned. "What have we here?"

Everyone zipped their lips and kept their eyes on the ground. Five quiet seconds ticked by before Robynne answered.

"A most unfortunate incident, sir. Sir Guy is dead."

The sheriff's eyes danced with glee, not at all congruous with his words. "Dead? What a pity."

"Yes, a real tragedy," Robynne went on without the slightest hint of sorrow.

"What happened?"

Willa looked at me, and I looked at Robynne.

"Well, it's hard to say," she said. "We only just happened upon this scene ourselves. But it seems his own men turned on him."

"You don't say," Daniel said dryly.

Robynne nodded sadly. "I can't imagine why..."

When Robert snickered, Alan kicked his shin.

"...but that's what we've been able to glean from the survivors. That's all we know, sadly."

"Sad, indeed." Daniel barely suppressed a grin.

"I suggest you assign your best men to investigate this terrible deed," Robynne added.

The sheriff's eyes sparkled with hidden laughter. "Oh, I will. The very best."

I could imagine it already: Nottingham's stupidest guards scratching their heads over the mysterious circumstances of Sir Guy's passing.

Over the past few months, I'd been congratulating our little band on a steady stream of successes. Only now did I realize the extent to which the sheriff had played a role in that. A dangerous role, and a selfless one. If he were exposed...

I let out a slow breath, more impressed by Daniel's courage than ever.

All that time, I'd only really considered my own small part of the picture. Now, I saw the extent of it all and the way we were all connected.

I squeezed Willa's hand. None of us was really safe until we were all safe. None would enjoy a happily-ever-after until we finished what we'd started — together.

I shook my head, chiding myself. How foolish I'd been to think I couldn't — or shouldn't — depend on others. Without their help, I would never have found — or won over — Willa. And without my full commitment, none of us would find peace. Not in Sherwood Forest, not in Nottingham, not anywhere.

As heavy as that thought was, Willa's touch was light and encouraging. Her eyes met mine, telegraphing a world of emotions. Among them, something like *We'll find a way. I swear we will.*

I took a deep breath. Yes, we would.

"Well, we must be going," Robynne announced breezily.

The horse's harness jingled, and the stallion perked his ears.

"You must, indeed," the sheriff agreed. "Though, I must ask who you are. For the record, of course."

The men froze. Willa held her breath. I gripped my staff harder.

"They call me Daisy," Robynne replied without the slightest hesitation.

Everyone, from me to the men and even the sheriff, stifled their laughter.

"Well then, Daisy. . ." The sheriff tipped an imaginary hat, emphasizing that made-up name. "I hope we meet again. In better circumstances, perhaps."

Robynne's eyes locked with his, showing a blend of humor and sorrow.

"Soon, I hope," Robynne murmured softly.

"The sooner, the better," Daniel agreed.

They locked eyes a moment longer then turned away with visible effort. The sheriff moved toward the city, while Robynne stepped toward the forest. One by one, we fell into step behind her. When we reached the edge of the trees, Robynne stopped and waved us forward.

"You all go ahead. I'll just take one minute. You know, to, uh. . ."

She hid it well, but I could sense how weary she was and how full of sorrow.

"To check no one follows us?" I filled in. "Good idea."

Robynne shot me a grateful look, and I pointed the men forward. "Go on, then. To camp, everyone. We'll see you there, Robynne."

"See you there," she murmured, gazing back toward Nottingham.

My eyesight wasn't as keen as Alan's, but I would bet anything Daniel stood at the city gates, gazing toward Robynne with just as much yearning.

∞∞∞∞

I kept going back to that image over the next few days. Every time I held Willa, I reminded myself how lucky I was. Not just to have found her, but in circumstances that allowed us to be together.

Not that it was entirely smooth sailing, of course.

"A mating *what*?" Willa hollered when I finally filled her in on that detail.

We were in my den, but her voice boomed out over the entire camp, and the guys didn't stop teasing for days.

Well, they tried teasing Willa — once. But one killer look from her shut them all up.

"No sense of humor," Robert muttered. "You're worse than Robynne,"

"I'll take that as a compliment." Willa glared.

They continued to tease me mercilessly — and quietly, lest Willa charged in to give them a piece of her mind. But much like the teasing about my name, I shrugged it off. All they had was teasing. I had true love.

It did take a hell of a lot of explaining, though.

"A mating bite. A little like getting married, but for shifters," I explained.

"All I have to do to get married is say *I do*," Willa grumbled. "No biting necessary."

Explaining that it was better than marriage — not just a few words and a piece of paper, but a true bond that lasted forever — took a lot of work too. But when I got to the part about her biting me back, her eyes sparkled.

Of course, she hid that with another grumble. "Why didn't you say so in the first place?"

Clearly, we were holding true to our promise to keep driving each other crazy — in a good way.

We decided not to rush things, but on our fourth night together, slow, sweet sex quickly spiraled into uncontrollable desire, and before I knew it, our bodies were locked in a frenzied, primal dance. Willa wrapped her legs around me, meeting every one of my thrusts with her own buck. Her hair was a wild mess, and her body glistened with sweat.

"Yes... More..." she urged.

I didn't have *more* to give her, even with my not-so-little... er, equipment. But when instinct made me scrape my teeth over her neck, Willa pressed closer.

"Yes... There..."

I blinked. That was where the mating bite went. Was the instinct that guided me leading her too?

I ran my teeth over that spot again, groaning with the effort it took to hold back. Then I found Willa's eyes and waited for her okay.

"Hell yes. Okay!" she growled.

Her lean body lined up perfectly with mine, and the heat we generated could have warmed the entire camp if we'd had some means to channel it that way.

"Okay to a bite?" I double-checked, although I was about to explode.

"I might die if you don't. So, yes. Yes, yes, yes!"

A chorus of furry bear angels sang in my mind. I let my fangs extend, then plunged them deep.

I felt a brief flash of pain, then wave upon wave of ecstasy. My vision went totally white, and my mind exploded with sensation — not only mine, but hers too.

I didn't just feel Willa arch under me — I felt the shock and pleasure from her point of view too. I sensed her pulse beat a hair away from my teeth, and I felt the hard edge of my fangs the way she registered them — welcomed them, even. I reveled in the throb of my hard shaft, buried deep, and I went dizzy with the rapture Willa felt. Every sensation I felt was echoed from her point of view, thanks to the mental connection created by the bite.

So good... Willa groaned in my mind.

I rolled my hips, making her cry out for more. *More* I managed to provide until we both exploded at the very same time.

An experience words couldn't fully capture. Suffice to say, her fingernail marks decorated my back and her cries of *Yes... More... Oh!* echoed in my ears for days.

A good thing we'd holed up in the deepest part of my den that night. We would never have heard the end of it if her cries had carried through camp.

Our den, my bear corrected me. *Ours and Willa's.*

We lay panting for a long time afterward, with Willa curled cozily in my arms in my favorite position — her back to my front. Her favorite position, too, as a peek into her mind confirmed.

"Wait. You can read my mind?" She went stiff.

I chuckled, because what I saw there was all good. Well, some of it was on the dirty side, but that was fine with me.

"And you can read mine. See?"

I pictured her straddling me, her pert breasts in reach of my lips, her chin tipped back in as she rode me wildly. Then I pictured her leaning in, her teeth extending...

Heat blazed through her body, assuring me the image came through crystal clear. Her heart beat a little faster under my hand, even if all she murmured was a quiet, "I see."

Then she turned in my arms and stuck an accusing finger at my chest. "Wait a minute. Those were your bear teeth, weren't they?"

I went still, keeping my lips sealed.

She tapped them insistently. "All right, mister. Open up. Show-and-tell."

I ran my tongue over my teeth, making sure they were back to their human size, then let her see.

"Oh no, you don't. Those were your bear teeth I felt."

"Human teeth don't reach far enough. So I had to extend my bear fangs," I explained very quietly.

She mulled that over, then tapped my lips again. "Show me."

I groaned. She'd already made me shift back and forth a dozen times in the past few days. At first, she'd been wary, but that had quickly given way to curiosity and wonder. She'd stroked the soft fur around my ears, studied my snout from every angle, and even squeezed my paws to make the claws extend. When she was finished, Willa gulped, then petted my paw.

Uh, thanks. Wow. Very big. All she'd managed to stammer was a string of monosyllabic words.

Gradually, she'd gotten used to the sight of me in bear form. So, why the obsession with teeth now?

Still, I knew better than to argue with my mate. I pulled back my lips and showed her my teeth, letting them slowly extend.

Willa's eyes went wide.

"Oh," she murmured, a little dazed. "Wow."

Yes, letting her draw her own conclusions was always best.

I went back to the vision of her riding me, then extending her own teeth for the bite, and...

I closed my eyes, surrendering to the fantasy. Hoping Willa liked what she saw too.

A moment later, she slid over my body and whispered in my ear. "Like this?"

Her voice was low and sultry, making me hard all over again.

"Exactly," I murmured breathlessly as she straddled me and teased with her hips.

I groaned as she took me in, one hard inch at a time.

She tipped her head back, just like in the fantasy, and started to rock over me. Her hips squeezed against mine, erasing any hint of separation. Then I groaned again, because she was leaning forward...licking my neck...nibbling...

I was in heaven, but a moment later, Willa broke away, frustrated.

"I can't believe I'm saying this, but I would give anything for fangs right now."

I laughed, making her body jerk.

"I can even see them." She closed her eyes and ran her tongue over her teeth. "I can practically feel them."

"Soon, my love," I promised, tugging her down for a kiss.

I'd explained that my mating bite would make her a shifter too, though I'd heard the process varied.

"How soon?" she groaned.

Patience was not my mate's strong suit. When she wanted something, she wanted it. And at that moment, she wanted me. Bad.

My bear side glowed.

"Soon," I promised, diving into a possessive kiss.

I ran my tongue over her teeth, then moaned as she did the same. What a high it was to witness her last apprehensions about shifters give way to delight — and desire.

She leaned to one side, rolling until we were back where we'd started.

"Can we do it again?" she asked, though I sensed *No* wasn't an option. Not that I was about to deny my mate. "I mean, can you bite me again?" she went on. "Just to tide me over until I can bite back."

I laughed, pulled her leg tight against my side, and thrust in hard.

"Happy to oblige, my mate."

I wish I could say I uttered those words casually, but they were more of a choked, needy cry. Willa didn't seem to mind, though. Moments later, at the height of sex, I scraped my teeth over her neck, and she cried into my mind.

Yes. Yes, please.

For the second time that night, I plunged my fangs deep, then tumbled into a hurricane of sensations I never wanted to end. Even when my breath ran out, forcing me to break off the bite, my body tingled. Eventually, we fell back, panting hard. I held Willa close, listening to her heart pound.

"Oh. My. God. If I'd known it was going to be that good..." she murmured.

I chuckled into her hair. I'd been skeptical that mating bites were overhyped. But now...

Definitely not hype, my bear hummed dreamily.

Then she sighed. "Now I owe you. Two bites."

I shook my head, then nodded. "No. I mean, yes. I mean, no more keeping score, remember?"

That was one lesson I'd learned for good. The key to a satisfied life wasn't counting how many times I offered or accepted help. What mattered was doing the right thing, no matter where the balance lay in the end.

Willa frowned, then brightened. "Oh. Does that mean I get to bite you as often as I want — or at least, as often as you want?"

I laughed and pulled her into a firm hug. "I want. Believe me, I want."

Chapter Twenty-One

JOHN

Another two days passed. Willa and I mostly kept to ourselves, surrendering to insatiable desire and slowly settling into a new life. We also helped with chores around camp, although after all the action of the past week, everyone had agreed to take it easy for a few days. Even Robynne.

She and Willa spent time together too, discussing who knows what. Girl talk, maybe — though for those two, *girl talk* probably included combat tactics, the latest trends in weaponry, and the challenges of leading a group of unruly men.

Our gang didn't have a strict hierarchy, but Robynne was top dog, and I was happy to be her left-hand man. Like Robynne, Willa had a sense of humor, but she didn't tolerate any nonsense from the men — including me — even when we were in animal form.

I chuckled, recalling the time Willa had stuck her hands on her hips and berated everyone.

"All right, who's been peeing on this tree? Seriously, people. The forest is full of trees. Is it too much to ask to call this area off-limits?"

Her blazing eyes dared anyone to object. Of course, no one did. Especially not Robert, who slunk silently away.

So, it didn't take Willa long to establish herself as a leading figure in the pack. And that was before she'd even started shifting! I couldn't wait to see her assert her natural authority as a bear. Thank goodness she and I had fallen into a balanced give-and-take, with me taking the lead on some things and her on others — all without keeping a tally.

Five days after the fight at the Sentinels, Robynne declared it time for a trip into Nottingham, which made our camp buzz with talk and activity. Even the dogs — including Nosewise, who'd fully integrated himself by then — joined in, trotting around and wagging their tails excitedly.

"Not sure that's a good idea," I murmured to Robynne.

Even my headstrong, *I fear nothing and nobody* mate agreed. "Maybe let a little more time pass."

But Robynne was adamant, and her eyes sparkled with some hidden plan.

"No better time than right now, I assure you. I'll just make a quick detour to Winslow Abbey first..."

She didn't explain why, and we knew better than to ask. We could only wait to find out what her scheming mind had come up with once the deed was done.

I usually accompanied Robynne on trips to town, but we agreed the risk of my being recognized was too high.

"You're just too big," Robynne said apologetically.

As if that was a bad thing.

"Willa can be the judge of that," Martin joked, making everyone roar in laughter. "What do you say, Willa?"

She blushed a little but held her ground. "A proper lady never talks." Everyone groaned in disappointment until she piped up a moment later. "Good thing I'm not a proper lady." Everyone cheered, then let her go on. "As for size, you know what they say. The man who is most obsessed with it is usually the least endowed."

Everyone howled at Martin, caught in his own joke. Even Robynne. But when she cleared her throat a moment later, signaling, *That was a good one, but that's enough now,* everyone settled down.

"Also, Martin has just volunteered himself to go with me," Robynne added with a grin.

Martin sighed as more hoots sounded.

"Alan, will you come too?" Robynne asked.

We accompanied them to the edge of the woods, where they shifted and set off, clothes bundled in their mouths or talons.

Willa stared a little at the fox, eagle, and badger that headed off, darting across fields and blending into hedgerows or soaring overhead.

"Wow."

Her whisper held a hint of yearning, and my bear side nearly cheered.

She likes us. She can't wait to be like us.

I couldn't wait either, but life was good as it was.

Still, worry sat in the pit of my stomach, as it always did when members of our clan ventured into town. We watched long after Robynne and the others disappeared in the direction of Winslow Abbey.

Ah, the abbey, Willa whispered in my mind. She wasn't shifting yet, but she had already mastered that shifter trick. *Maybe we can visit sometime. Check out the millhouse. . .*

I coughed to cover up my bear's lusty growl. Yes, the millhouse would forever be a special place, if an unexpected one.

We cut through the forest to the point closest to Nottingham to await Robynne's return. On the way, we crossed the very brook where Willa and I had once faced off.

Willa shot me a secret smile. *Remember that day?*

I grinned. I would never forget.

Then we settled in with a view of the Sentinels to wait. And wait. . .

Smoke curled out of the chimney roofs in the distance, and the sun gradually made its way past its low winter zenith.

"What's taking so long?" Robert asked.

I had started to worry too when a little band appeared on the trail out of town. When they came closer, we all gaped.

"Wow. I shouldn't be surprised, but this one takes the cake," Robert murmured.

I had to agree, because when Robynne and the others finally entered the woods, they did so with a huge, creaky hay wagon pulled by two mules and one surprise guest.

"What the. . . ?" I started.

Tuck held the reins in one hand and raised a goblet of ale in the other.

"Finally, I get to see Sherwood Forest for myself!"

We all stared as they rolled along the bumpy forest track.

"Well, don't just stand there. Come along!" Robynne admonished. "We'll need help unloading this hay."

"Hay?" Robert blinked once we got into camp. "What do we need hay for?"

Tuck indicated the mules. "For Rita and Rosie, of course."

Robert scratched his head. "What do we need Rita and Rosie for?"

Tuck traded amused grins with Robynne. "Help us unload and you'll see. It starts with a keg of the abbey's best beer..." He tapped the wooden barrel, eliciting a cheer. "And continues to even greater surprises."

I hopped up to help, but Willa stood frozen.

"What?" I asked, tossing down a bale of hay.

Willa's jaw hung open before she murmured, "Hay...from the stables..."

"That's usually where they keep it," Robert teased, hopping up to help.

Tuck jumped down from the wagon and offered each of the mules a handful of hay. "You see, ladies? Just because we've been kidnapped doesn't mean we don't get fed."

So that was how Robynne had extracted Tuck from the abbey — kidnapping. Not that he would have put up any resistance.

Robert tossed down another bale of hay, then knocked on a hidden crate. "What's this?"

Robynne grinned. "Have a look."

"More beer?" Robert asked hopefully.

Tuck chewed on the end of a straw. "Not exactly."

Robert cleared away more straw, exposing a wooden trunk that looked familiar. Then he froze, staring. "Oh. My. Lord."

I recognized the trunk at the very same moment. I glanced at Willa, who grinned at Robynne. The others motioned at Robert impatiently.

"What is it, already?"

Robert reached in, then held up something big and shiny for all to see. A silver goblet. Next, he produced a jewel-encrusted necklace, and after that, a cross studded with diamonds.

"The treasure! You recovered the treasure!" Willa cheered.

Robynne nodded in satisfaction as everyone raced closer for a look. "We did, including what you hid in the rafters, just where you described. You can send word to your mistress that it's safe in the forest, as she intended."

For a few minutes, everyone milled around, marveling at the treasure.

"Where did you find it?" someone asked.

"The stables," Robynne and Willa said at the same time. They blinked at each other, then broke out laughing.

"I'd almost given up hope of recovering it," Willa added.

Robynne shook her head, and her gaze drifted into the distance. "Never give up hope."

A lump formed in my throat at the double meaning for her.

"It has to be worth a fortune!" old Christopher marveled.

Willa nodded. "Not enough to pay the king's ransom, maybe, but a good portion of it."

"A very significant portion," Robynne agreed. Then she pointed sternly at the men. "You get tonight to admire it. Then, as Willa's mistress intended, it all joins the loot we've been saving."

Robert whistled, still amazed by it all. "She must be the richest lady in the kingdom."

"Who is it, Willa?" Alan asked.

"Yes. Who is it?" everyone begged. Even Robynne tilted her head at Willa.

She hedged a while before hinting, "Someone close to the king."

"Judging by this loot, she's a goddamn princess," Robert muttered.

"Come on, Willa," the men pleaded.

Robynne stuck up a hand. "If the owner wished to remain anonymous, we must respect that."

Willa considered. "I suppose it's all right for me to say. Her plan was for everyone to know she was robbed, so she wouldn't be suspected by Prince John and his supporters. Of course, her true intention was for the treasure to land here, among those loyal to the king."

I ran my hands through my hair. God, what a roundabout voyage that treasure had taken — all due to my own stupidity.

Not stupidity, my bear murmured. *Destiny. Thanks to everything that happened, we have the treasure* and* Willa.*

Willa smiled at me, then finally relented to the men's badgering. "She's the king's goddaughter."

Everyone looked blank. We all came from humble backgrounds with little knowledge — or interest — in high society.

But Tuck's mouth hung open. "You're kidding."

Ah, leave it to Tuck — as the only one among us who came from a noble family, he was familiar with the who's who of the upper class.

"Come on, Tuck," everyone cried. "Tell us, already."

He shook his head, still getting over the shock, then looked at Willa. "You work for Maid Marian?"

Everyone gasped — even me, and at least three different voices chimed in with the same words at the same time.

"The most beautiful woman in the country?"

Willa rolled her eyes, and Robynne kicked the ground, muttering, "Men!"

"Is it her? Is it really?" the men asked.

Willa nodded.

"Is she as beautiful as they say?" Robert asked.

Willa snorted, echoing Robynne. "Men!"

In their defense, Maid Marian did have a hell of a reputation — one I doubted anyone could live up to. Not that I cared. Character and brains trumped beauty, and anyway, Willa had all three.

Tuck raised his goblet. "Three cheers for the good Maid Marian. May we someday have the pleasure of drinking to her in person."

All the men snickered. "I'll be the first in line."

Soon, we had the treasure — and hay — unloaded. Martin started a crackling bonfire, warming a roast pig, and the ale started flowing. Everyone gathered, laughing, eating, and trading stories until late into the night.

I sat to one side with Willa in the scoop of my arms, only half tuned in to the others. We had a lot to celebrate — from Robynne's return to Willa's escape, the demise of Sir Guy, and recovering the treasure — but I felt like the greatest winner. I had my mate.

Willa grinned at that but gradually grew pensive. "I wish I could promise it will all be smooth sailing, but considering how much evil is still out there..."

I followed her gaze to the shadows beyond the dancing campfire.

"At least we're rid of Sir Guy," I pointed out.

"True," she agreed, then sighed. "I have to wonder where the evil in him came from. Was it a by-product of his upbringing, or was cruelty in his blood?"

Robynne, sitting near us, frowned. "In his blood..."

My body chilled as I caught her meaning.

"What?" Willa asked.

Robynne and I looked at each other, but she was the first to speak.

"Sir Guy has a sister. And whether it's the upbringing or the genes, I've heard Lady Thornton is just as bad, Maybe worse."

The others weren't listening, which was just as well. They deserved one carefree evening. But the three of us sat pensively, each lost in our own thoughts.

"At least we have this. Here. I meant to give it to you." Willa pulled a ring from her pocket and handed it to Robynne.

She turned it over, curious. "Something tells me it's not just a pretty piece of jewelry."

Willa shook her head. "My mistress sent two special pieces with the treasure. The spelled dagger was one..."

That, we'd already hidden in a secret cache. It was a great weapon, but an equally great danger — even to Willa, now that she'd started her gradual transformation to bear shifter.

"...and this ring was the other," Willa continued. "It's the Ring of Aquitaine, a gift from King Richard to my mistress. It belonged to his mother, Eleanor of Aquitaine."

Robynne looked duly impressed, and I was too. Eleanor of Aquitaine was ahead of her time — a powerful queen in her own right who'd personally led armies in the Crusades.

"Marian said the ring gives its bearer extraordinary powers, and I believe it," Willa continued. "But only if the bearer is a woman. So, we need to keep it safe from the likes of Lady Thornton." Her voice faltered. "Maybe even from ourselves."

Robynne nodded slowly, frowning. "We'll keep it safe until we hear from your mistress."

Willa looked relieved but pensive. "I should send her a message soon."

"Soon," I agreed.

We stared quietly off into the fire while the others continued to revel. Tuck was one of the loudest, making the most of his rare chance to party.

"Poor guy," Willa observed. "He's really not cut out for a monastery."

"No, he isn't," I agreed. "But you never know about destiny..."

Willa laughed. "Now, that would be something. Finding Tuck some way out of there."

Robynne chuckled, though her words were earnest. "Not too soon, I hope. He's too useful to us where he is." Then her eyes dimmed, and she stared deeper into the fire.

Too useful where he is... I mulled that over. It applied equally to Daniel, the sheriff.

The fire snapped and crackled, leading my thoughts in similarly random, swirling directions. Would Robynne and Daniel ever get a chance to enjoy small moments like this? Laughing, drinking, making merry with friends around a fire? And what about Tuck? Would he ever escape that prison of an existence? My eyes landed on Robert next, and my bear snorted.

Will he ever grow up and develop some intelligence?

I smiled in spite of myself. Robynne said to never give up hope, but in Robert's case... Well, I wouldn't hold my breath.

But when it came to Robynne, Daniel, Tuck, and even King Richard — heck, when it came to the future of the country, I had to hope. More importantly, I had to play my part in achieving the peace we all strove for.

Willa turned in my arms to make eye contact. Her emerald eyes were glowing — a sure sign of her inner beast awakening.

She patted my hands, smiled, and repeated what she'd vowed that night at the Sentinels.

We'll find a way. I swear we will. Not just for us, but for the others.

I tucked my chin next to hers and hugged her closer. Yes, we would. Whatever it took, and however long it took. I swore we'd help achieve peace for us all. Somehow.

∞∞∞∞

Dear reader,

I hope you enjoyed this second book in the Sherwood Forest Shifters trilogy. I know you're dying for Robynne and Daniel to get their happily-ever-after too, and it's coming soon — I promise! I feel the same way, but the situation in Nottingham doesn't yet allow them to expose their love or their support for King Richard. I assure you, they will finally unite once the events of Book 3 play out.

However, you (and they) can get some instant gratification by reading Private Investigation, *the bonus scene to* Tempting the Outlaw. *That's told from Daniel's point of view and will update you on what happened to Robynne and Daniel during their absence from Nottingham and Sherwood Forest.* Private Investigation *and dozens of other bonus scenes are available exclusively to subscribers of Anna Lowe's newsletter. You can find the sign up link on www.annalowebooks.com.*

After that, read Tempting the Maiden, *Book 3, the grand finale of this series, in which Robynne and Daniel get their full happily-ever-after. Tuck finally gets his love story too, but as you can guess, it won't be easy for him. Don't miss* Tempting the Maiden! *Happy reading!*

Sneak Peek: Tempting the Maiden

He was born to be a knight. I'm a noble lady. We're a perfect match — but destiny has other ideas...

MARIAN

Fairest maiden in the land? I'd rather be known as the best swordswoman or the best rider. On the other hand, there are advantages to keeping my skills secret — along with my rare shifter heritage. Like now, when I must outwit the cruelest, most ruthless man alive. To do so, I head to the most lawless corner of the country, hoping to find Robin Hood. But when the safe haven I was counting on turns out to be a double cross, I find an unlikely ally in the hottest priest in the land...

TUCK

As the third son of a country lord, I had no choice but to join a monastery. *Eat, pray, repeat* was my future, and damn, was that future bleak. In a few short days, I'll have to take my vows and make it official. Me, a lion shifter, living a life of poverty, obedience, and chastity?

Life gets a little more interesting when I start helping Robynne Hood... and a LOT more interesting when a beautiful and mysterious noblewoman comes to our monastery, seeking refuge. I'm her only hope, but it would take a miracle to earn a happily-ever-after. I'll have to settle for saving her from greedy, ruthless shifters plotting to overthrow the monarchy — if she'll even let me. Still, I've always been a dreamer, and I'm not ready to give up hope, love, or the chance to fulfill my true destiny.

Books by Anna Lowe

Sherwood Forest Shifters

Tempting the Sheriff (Book 1)

Tempting the Outlaw (Book 2)

Tempting the Maiden (Book 3)

Aloha Shifters - Jewels of the Heart

Lure of the Dragon (Book 1)

Lure of the Wolf (Book 2)

Lure of the Bear (Book 3)

Lure of the Tiger (Book 4)

Love of the Dragon (Book 5)

Lure of the Fox (Book 6)

Aloha Shifters - Pearls of Desire

Rebel Dragon (Book 1)

Rebel Bear (Book 2)

Rebel Lion (Book 3)

Rebel Wolf (Book 4)

Rebel Heart (A prequel to Book 5)

Rebel Alpha (Book 5)

Fire Maidens - Billionaires & Bodyguards

Fire Maidens: Paris (Book 1)

Fire Maidens: London (Book 2)

Fire Maidens: Rome (Book 3)

Fire Maidens: Portugal (Book 4)

Fire Maidens: Ireland (Book 5)

Fire Maidens: Scotland (Book 6)

Fire Maidens: Venice (Book 7)

Fire Maidens: Greece (Book 8)

Fire Maidens: Switzerland (Book 9)

The Wolves of Twin Moon Ranch

Desert Hunt (the Prequel)

Desert Moon (Book 1)

Desert Blood (Book 2)

Desert Fate (Book 3)

Desert Heart (Book 4)

Desert Rose (Book 5)

Desert Roots (Book 6)

Desert Destiny (Book 7)

Sasquatch Surprise (Book 8)

Desert Yule (a short story)

Desert Wolf: Complete Collection (Four short stories)

Blue Moon Saloon

Perfection (a short story prequel)

Damnation (Book 1)

Temptation (Book 2)

Redemption (Book 3)

Salvation (Book 4)

Deception (Book 5)

Celebration (a holiday treat)

Shifters in Vegas

Paranormal romance with a zany twist

Gambling on Trouble

Gambling on Her Dragon

Gambling on Her Bear

Gambling on Her Panther

Serendipity Adventure Romance

Off the Charts

Uncharted

Entangled

Windswept

Adrift

Travel Romance

Veiled Fantasies

Island Fantasies

www.annalowebooks.com

About the Author

USA Today and Amazon bestselling author Anna Lowe loves putting the "hero" back into heroine and letting location ignite a passionate romance. She likes a heroine who is independent, intelligent, and imperfect – a woman who is doing just fine on her own. But give the heroine a good man – not to mention a chance to overcome her own inhibitions – and she'll never turn down the chance for adventure, nor shy away from danger.

Anna loves dogs, sports, and travel – and letting those inspire her fiction. On any given weekend, you might find her hiking in the mountains or hunched over her laptop, working on her latest story. Either way, the day will end with a chunk of dark chocolate and a good read.

Visit AnnaLoweBooks.com

9 781958 597538